THE ANNIVERSARY

and Other Stories

Also by Louis Auchincloss

❀

THE ANNIVERSARY

and Other Stories

LOUIS AUCHINCLOSS

Houghton Mifflin Company

Boston   New York

1999

LIBRARY OF CONGRESS CATALOGING-IN-PUBLICATION DATA

Auchincloss, Louis.
The anniversary and other stories / Louis Auchincloss.
p.   cm.
Contents: DeCicco v. Schweizer — The interlude — The anniversary
— Man of the Renaissance — The last of the great courtesans —
The devil and Guy Lansing — The facts of fiction —
The Virgina redbird — The veterans.
ISBN 0-395-97074-1
1. United States — Social life and customs — 20th
century — Fiction.   I. Title.
PS3501.U25A74   1999   813'.54 — dc21
99-18697   CIP

Book design by Anne Chalmers
Typeface: Granjon with Cochin display

PRINTED IN THE UNITED STATES OF AMERICA

QUM 10 9 8 7 6 5 4 3 2 1

For my granddaughter,

ELIZABETH MARVEL AUCHINCLOSS

CONTENTS

THE ANNIVERSARY

and Other Stories

DeCicco v. Schweizer

Prologue

WHEN I ENROLLED in the University of Virginia Law School in the autumn of 1938, I had resolved to abandon forever my early abortive attempts to write fiction and devote myself heart and soul to the rigors of my new profession. And for a while I was faithful to that purpose. But I soon discovered a siren on the banks of the new river on which I paddled that drew me ineluctably back to the muse I had sought to forsake. The lyrics of the siren's song were the mellifluous prose of Benjamin Cardozo, whose common law opinions from his Albany bench were then generally received by the bar as the finest-wrought statements of jurisprudence that we had — excepting only those of Marshall and Holmes. Cardozo's reputation has not gone without sharp challenge in our own day, but I impenitently remain the disciple I became in 1938.

I had taken, at the start of my legal studies, the arbitrary and immature position that there was no true meeting point between law and literature, that the former was dry and practical and part of the world of economic profit to which men, average men anyway, had to bind themselves, and that the latter was a fantasy of color and delight, the plaything of the intellectually privileged, of those rare geniuses whose talent exempted them from the toil of the masses. When Cardozo, however, in the opinions that I now studied, would outline the tissue of events that had resulted in the litigation before him and fit them into the golden straitjacket of law, I found myself wonderfully returned to the world of my favorite masters of American fiction: the world of Hawthorne, of Dreiser, of Edith Wharton, even of Henry James.

I was particularly drawn to the case of *DeCicco v. Schweizer*, perhaps because it was a case in contracts, which had become my favorite course. The facts were these: on January 2, 1902, one Joseph Schweizer instructed his attorney to draw up and deliver to his daughter, Blanche, and her betrothed, Count Gulinelli of Ferrara, a document in which he committed himself to pay Blanche an annuity of $2500 commencing on the day of her marriage. Four days later the couple were wed, and the sum due was presumably paid each year until 1912 when the plaintiff, one DeCicco, to whom the document had been assigned by the count and countess, presented it to Schweizer, who refused payment on the ground that no "consideration" had been paid him for his promise. Consideration, as every first-year law student promptly learns, is the *quid pro quo* that makes a promise enforceable at law. If nothing is given to him who makes the offer, nothing can be required of him. But Cardozo and his fellow judges found for the plaintiff on the ground that Blanche and her betrothed had indeed given her father something in exchange for his offer: they had chosen not to exercise their undoubted privilege to break their engagement and had fulfilled at the altar the condition that activated his commitment.

It didn't matter that they may have never wished or intended to break their troth, or that they may have regarded themselves as morally bound to fulfill it, or even that Schweizer may never have meant them to feel they had to go through with a ceremony unless both were so inclined. The fact remained that Blanche's father had promised to pay his money on a certain condition, and that this condition had been met by the two promisees who had been free not to meet it.

Cardozo's opinion offered a good example of his literary style:

> He [Schweizer] offered this inducement to both while they were free to retract or to delay. That they neither retracted nor delayed is certain. It is not to be expected that they should lay bare all the motives and promptings, some avowed and conscious, others perhaps half-conscious and inarticulate, which swayed their conduct. It is enough that the natural consequence of the defendant's promise was to induce them to put the thought of rescission or delay aside. . . . It will not do to divert the minds of others from a given line of conduct, and then to urge that because of the diversion the opportunity has gone by to say how their minds might otherwise have acted. If the tendency of the promise is to induce them to persevere, reliance and detriment may be inferred from the mere act of performance. The springs of conduct are subtle and varied. One who meddles with them must not insist upon too nice a measure of proof that the spring which he released was effective to the exclusion of all others.

Did not fiction and law come together in this opinion, not as antagonists (as I had foolishly once viewed them), but rather as partners to investigate and even make sense out of the human condition? For if the court had the job of deciding whether the plaintiff DeCicco should collect on his assignment (even though one suspects he purchased it at a fearful discount), is not the novelist concerned with the "motives and promptings" of human conduct, some avowed, some only half conscious, the subtle and varied "springs of conduct," which the court must ignore? To each his own. But Cardozo might have been a novelist himself. Indeed, had he had a better writer as a tutor in his boyhood than the later famed Horatio Alger, perhaps he might!

The marriage of American heiresses to European noblemen was a common enough social phenomenon of Blanche Schweizer's era, often romanticized and just as often deplored in the press, in fiction, in plays and, ultimately, on the screen. In fiction the most elegant and lacquered example is found in James's *The Golden Bowl*, which deals with the marriage of Maggie Verver, most opulent of American heiresses, and Prince Amerigo, noblest of Italian peers. The shabby little facts of the Schweizer case seem a long way from the glittering world of *The Golden Bowl*, but in Cardozo's opinion the principle of law that emerges from them is like refined steel from crude ore.

I know nothing of the facts of the case other than what is set down in the opinion. Did the marriage last? We know that Blanche and her husband executed the assignment a decade after their wedding, but we do not know whether they were still happily joined. They must have been hard pressed financially to have been reduced to that extreme. And why had the annuity been offered at all, only four days before the wedding? Was Gulinelli threatening to pull out? Yet he must have been really broke if he would marry for so small a sum, even considering its greater purchasing power in 1902. Or had the offer been an addition to a previously made settlement? Was it possible that Blanche was using a last-minute ploy to extract an additional sum from her father by threatening her mother with the disgrace of a cancelled wedding now that the invitations were out and the presents in? Or had Schweizer, beaming over a recent coup in the market, been moved to crown any previous gifts with a final one?

I had eventually to satisfy my curiosity about the Schweizer case in the only way a novelist can, by making up my own version, and that is what follows. I set it in the form of Blanche's memoirs, penned in her old age, after the other principals of her story were dead:

Now It Can Be Told

AN EXCERPT FROM
THE FORTHCOMING AUTOBIOGRAPHY OF
COUNTESS BLANCHE GULINELLI

Style Magazine, August 1955

NOTHING IS MORE COMMON, in probing the shadowy background of childhood, than for a writer to overemphasize the role of her parents — and, particularly in American lives, that of the mother. *Cherchez la mère* is the inevitable cry. And far be it from me to say that the role of mine was not crucial, as I shall duly relate. But what is often overlooked in the backgrounds of the well-to-do, particularly in the America of the eighteen eighties and nineties when immigration had filled their households with cheap foreign help, is the importance of servants in whose care the children were so largely left. My governess, Miss Hankinson, an Englishwoman, daughter of a poor but very respectable curate, had been flung penniless on the world at his death, armed only with a bristling virtue, of which her angular spinster frame and long-nosed physiognomy gave her little need, an education centered in romantic poetry, particularly Lord Tennyson's, and a rock-ribbed social snobbishness. It was perfectly evident to me from the beginning of her lengthy tenure that she looked down on my parents, as well as their noisy friends and their pompous Beaux-Arts town house on Riverside Drive.

For, as Miss Hankinson could easily see, my family was not really "in society" at all, as our West Side residence alone would have told me had I been older. Mother was what was known as "a fine figure of a woman," certainly tall and handsome enough, unlike poor brown undersized me, whose sad looks and skinny body were the target of her constant sarcasms, but even my young eyes could make out that she was overdressed. It was probably her passion to dominate that led her to content herself with her Riverside group, but she certainly cast more than one resentful glance across Central Park to where Mrs. Astor held sway over a larger and more glittering domain. Things, however, were probably just as well as they were, for Mother's terrible tantrums would have constituted a definite hurdle in any attempt on her part to climb the ladders of Fifth Avenue or Newport. And then, too, we weren't nearly rich enough for that game. We lived lavishly, but we spent all we had and more.

Father had a temper equal to Mother's, but by some kind of tacit understanding, in the interest, perhaps, of a common survival, they seemed to have agreed that only one would "blow" at a time. He was large and red-faced and stentorian, at times rather ominously Germanic; he inclined to dress in loud British tweeds and to shout at servants and office clerks. His businesses were various; he was always in and out of things, investing in this or that, highly speculative, and one was never quite sure whether tomorrow would bring a diamond as big as the Ritz or a mail full of dunning letters. He treated me with a sometimes benign condescension unless he spotted something to criticize, and then he would bellow.

Miss Hankinson provided me with at least a simulacrum of the love that I missed in family life, and indeed she remained with me until she died, following me to Italy after my marriage and gallantly learning the language and adapting herself, as well as she could, to the shabby genteel poverty of our life in Ferrara. In some ways, however, it was the least she could do for me, as she, quite as much as my mother, though for very different reasons, was responsible for my ultimate agreement to marry Count Gulinelli. But before that time, alone and friend-less in her fifth-floor room on Riverside Drive, watching the winter wind ruffle the bleak Hudson, Hanky, as I called her, had given her whole heart to the little girl who seemed, in her own odd way, to be sharing her fate, while below my mother gaily entertained her loud friends at a glittering table laden with goodies and favors and sweets and decorated with a large silver sculptured group of Arion being rescued from a terrifying shark.

I went in the morning to a small private girls' school, but most of such learning as I acquired resulted from my afternoons and evenings with Hanky: large slices of Victorian verse and European history with emphasis on Great Britain's glorious as-similation of the globe. Hanky also kept a sacred scrapbook into which she lovingly pasted photographs of the royal family that she had cut out from magazines retrieved from the trash.

When we touched on the darker sides of history, such as the barbarian invasions of the Roman Empire, which Hanky saw as the splendid but doomed predecessor of Britain's, when she sighed over the lamentable spectacle of tall marble columns being toppled by hairy men in bearskins, I noted that she had begun to emphasize the survival of Rome in some of the great families of the Renaissance: the Medici, the Dorias, the Estes. I asked her what this new promotion was all about, and she con-fessed that my mother had instructed her to teach me something about Italian nobility, as my parents were planning that I should accompany them on a trip to Tuscany.

"But since when did Mother care what *I* knew about the peo-ple she meets? Or hopes to meet?"

"I'm sure I don't know, dear. I do what I'm told. And I've had to read whole chapters of John Addington Symonds!"

"Well, I'd much rather learn about the barbarians." I knew how to get poor Hanky's goat, and though I loved her I could never resist it. "Do you think the Kaiser might be the modern Attila? Born to bring the British Empire down?"

Hanky sniffed. "He'll have the Royal Navy to contend with! That should give him pause!"

"And perhaps he'd have too much respect for his grand-mother to think of invading the country she rules!"

I knew that to Hanky this blood tie was the supreme irony of modern history.

"It wouldn't be his English blood that would stop him! He never had the advantage of a good English education."

"English blood? Surely Queen Victoria herself is entirely German?"

"But she was raised as an English princess."

"By a German governess." Hanky had taught me too well!

"But in an English court. Surrounded by English ladies and gentlemen."

Now how was it, my reader may ask, that, emotionally iso-lated as I was, I could so clearly see not only my parents as Hanky saw them but Hanky as my parents so condescendingly saw *her*? How was I able to stand back and correct the exagger-ations of each viewpoint? And how could I be so fond of Hanky and still see how silly she was? Or respect my mother for her force and willpower, even when I took in how faintly maternal she was, or dryly assessed the weakness of my father's bluster, even while I yearned for some share of his devotion?

I can only offer the explanation that the way I somehow man-aged to cope with a world that seemed to have so little place for me was to step out of it as far as I could and view it as a play or spectacle. And then judge it? Was that revenge, or simply a means of survival? At any rate I never took for granted that the world had to make sense. Or even that my life did.

It was through Enid Goldstein, a pretty but snotty girl in my class at school, a natural leader and inclined to be scornful of my dim looks and small stature, that I learned of my family's matrimonial plans for me. Enid's object in telling me (she never dreamt that I didn't know) was to assure me how little *she* was impressed by my mother's choice.

"I gather every other man in Wop Land is a count," she told me.

"But, Enid, I don't know what you're talking about."

"You really don't know? That your family's got an Italian nobleman picked out for you? Count Gulinelli. From Ferrara. My mother told me all about it. Your mother met him at a charity tea and was immediately swept off her feet."

"You mean *she* fell in love with him."

"Well, with his title, anyway. And his lovely old mortgaged palazzo. Mummie says your ma wants to emulate the Vanderbilts and Goulds and have a titled son-in-law."

It was too much for me. For a moment I could only gasp. "But," I cried when I had caught my breath, "I've heard Mother say a dozen times that this running after coronets was ridiculous. 'Un-American,' she called it. 'Typical Fifth Avenue.'"

"Well, I guess now she's decided it's time Riverside Drive had its own peerage. And *she* will be the pioneer!"

"But she can't *make* me marry him, can she?"

"No, but she can sure put the heat on you." Enid looked at me scornfully. "Do you think you can really stand up to her, Blanche? Even when she's backed by your old man?"

"Father? What does he care about Italian counts?"

"I hear from mine that he's up to his neck in a Venetian perfume deal. And he's hired the count as his front man to handle the Italians!"

My parents did not at once confirm Enid's prediction, but a week later Count Gulinelli was their guest at dinner, and I was seated next to him, which was not my customary place with a guest of honor, and he devoted more attention to me than I usually received from any man who had Mother on his other side. His manners, I admit, were good, perhaps too good, and his compliments elegant if on the florid side. He obviously meant little of what he said, but he made me think twice before condemning a social code that did things so prettily. He was not really handsome; he was too thin, too angular, too jerkily active, but he had sleek, glossy black hair, shiny eyes and a rather fine aquiline nose. He was approaching forty but seemed younger; idleness, at least until his employment by Father, had preserved his bloom.

Mother, as Enid had suggested, seemed obsessed with him. She could hardly spare his attentions to me, even though she had presumably requested them. She had learned a few phrases of Italian and embarrassed me by trotting them out showily. Though easily bored, she was the victim of sudden fads and crazes, and her new cosmopolitanism had hit her hard. The question immediately raised in my mind was: could I sit this one out, or would I be drowned in its first flood?

It did not take her long to make her intentions clear. After the count's second visit, she came to my room — a rare occurrence — when I was preparing for bed and settled herself in a chair for what she termed "a cozy chat."

"What did you think of the count, child?"

I knew her methods well enough to be sure there was no use pussyfooting around the main issue. "That depends. As a friend or as a husband?"

"What on earth makes you ask that?"

"Enid Goldstein's mother says you want him for a son-in-law."

To watch Mother try to cope with the fit of temper to which she usually at once gave in was a novel experience. "I wish those people would mind their own business! As if Sarah Goldstein wouldn't give her eyeteeth to snag the count for *her* daughter! But fat chance of *that*! If he's willing to overlook our being Lutherans, he'd certainly draw the line at a Jewess. But yes, I'll be frank with you. Your father and I *have* let the count know, in answer to his own most respectful plea, that we would have no objection if he presented himself as a suitor for your lily-white hand. Which doesn't mean, my dear, that you have to do anything but politely listen to him. We have made careful checks on his title, his background, his general reputation. There's not a spot on him anywhere. His character is amiable, his temper mild, his heart, I'm sure, in the right place. What more could a girl like you want?"

"I want to know why he wants me."

"A perfectly fair question." Oh, Mother had squarely faced the need of persuasion, an unfamiliar weapon in her armory. She knew that force, for once, might not be the way to prevail. "He feels the time has come for his old stock to have new blood introduced. For generations the Gulinellis have intermarried only with the oldest nobility —"

"He thinks I'll bring them vigor?"

Mother frowned. She hated irony, and my reference to my own skinny figure irritated her. "Well, you bear the genes of strength, anyway. Look at your father."

"And I suppose new blood really means new money." I was feeling even bolder as Mother continued to control her ire.

"Of course he expects your father to settle something on you! That's the European way. Even over here no young man, at least in *our* world, would take Joseph Schweizer's daughter without a penny. Only a fool would, and do you want to marry a fool? Let's face it, my dear. You're not exactly the catch of catches all by your lonesome."

"But suppose I don't want to marry at all?"

"You want to be an old maid? What sort of a life is that, even if you have money, and it's a question of how much of that you'll have, with the mad way your father plays the market? And think of the good life you'd have as a countess! Living in a fine old palazzo, with beautiful Italian bambinos, looked up to by the villagers, revered . . . oh, I wish I'd ever had half such a lark!"

"But aren't Italian husbands always unfaithful?"

"Did Enid tell you that?"

"No, I read it in the papers about that Vespucci divorce case."

"Hanky, I'll bet," Mother retorted scornfully. "That withered virgin lives for the tabloids. I should have given her the sack years ago. Well, yes. Italian men are not renowned for their fidelity. But that's because they're such great lovers. A wife sometimes has to take the bitter with the sweet. Many's the American girl who would prefer the Romeo who sometimes strays to the stout broker obsessed with market news and sports! Who may not look at another woman because he doesn't even know there's another woman to look at!"

It made me almost sorry for Mother to perceive that she was unconsciously contrasting the aridity of her own married life with her fantasy of what mine might be.

What she at last extracted from me was my agreement not wholly to close my mind to her proposition and to give the count the chance at least to try to make himself agreeable to me. I was still too unsophisticated to realize that with this concession I had already lost half the battle.

The count was now a frequent guest, and Mother always arranged, even when there were others at dinner, that he and I should sit together after the meal in a corner of the parlor where we could talk alone. He, of course, did most of the talking, and I will freely admit that he could be sufficiently entertaining with stories about his younger days in Ferrara. His tales were mild enough, it is true, and there was a quiet charm about them, a kind of subdued old-world nostalgia. I was not, however, in the least bit in love with him, nor he, certainly, with me.

A factor that worked more strongly in the count's favor was Hanky herself. Of course, she would have vastly preferred a hearty English peer, seen in her mind's eye clad in coronation robes with a picturesque old castle in the background, and she was no great enthusiast for Italians, whom she viewed as "a lesser breed" only too likely to be "without the law." But she drew a distinction between the latter and their nobility, fantasizing the count as a lineal descendant of the Caesars without any infusion of barbarian blood, and his assiduous little courtesies to her, if encountered in the hall or on the stairway, tipped the scale in his favor. But most of all I suspected that she yearned to liberate me — and herself, no doubt — from the Riverside world of my parents to what she must have imagined as the comparative bliss of an old Italian palazzo where the dower-bringing American bride would be received with a grateful respect. I was more skeptical than she, but her gentle and persistent optimism over the weeks had its effect.

The only person in active opposition to the count's suit was Enid Goldstein. I sometimes thought she was jealous of the prospect of my becoming the first girl in our school class to marry, and to marry a count at that, but there were other times when it occurred to me it might have been simple kindness.

"Gulinelli is absolutely bust," she assured me. "This job he's doing for your old man is the first steady income he's seen in years. Believe me, my mother knows all about it. The saying in Ferrara is that if the wolf was at their door, they'd eat him. And what's more, he's got an old Italian mama who rules the roost. You won't be able to call your soul your own!"

I don't know how Mother discovered what Enid had told me,

but she stormed into my room one night to deny it and show me pictures of the palazzo and its garden, which looked in prosperous shape, and a letter from an American vice-consul describing the old countess as bedridden, senile and utterly harmless. She then told me that she had forbidden Enid the house and that I was not to go to hers.

And so in the weeks that followed, increasingly watched and confined by my mother and the four Irish housemaids who were her staunch allies (like many imperious, egocentric women she was an excellent *maîtresse de maison*), isolated from a world in which I had few if any effective friends, seeing my Italian suitor as my sole chance of escape from a stifling existence, lulled by his mellifluous reassurances and armed with the knowledge that I could take Hanky with me in my new life, I at last gave in to my fate.

Mother was almost pleasant to me now, as she immersed herself in plans for a wedding that was to dazzle Riverside Drive. Father assured me smilingly that I should not be the loser — he had had, it appeared, a good year in the market — and Hanky beamed. But it was in my fiancé, "Oberto" as I was now to call him, that I noted the greatest change. He began to treat me in what strangely struck me as an almost fraternal manner, as if he and I were the innocent victims of a force far greater than ourselves to which we could only submissively bow our heads but about which, in lowered tones, even with an occasional smirk, we could humbly speak our minds.

It was in one such moment of confidence, in a stroll up the Drive — I was allowed to walk out now with him, unchaperoned — that he told me of the girl in Ferrara he had wanted to marry. He admitted, almost with pride, that they were still very much in love and that giving each other up was a shared sorrow. That it was necessary, however, he took quite for granted.

"But why shouldn't you have married her?" I protested.

"She hadn't a groat. What would we have lived on? My mother would never have allowed it. And her family had some rich burgher in mind for her."

"Did she marry him?"

"No, he backed out, at the last minute. Mother said it proved her point."

I recalled what my mother had told me of the harmlessness of the dowager Countess Gulinelli. So that was a lie too! "But that's terrible!" I exclaimed. "You ought to marry her now! Was there any other objection besides money?"

"Besides money! You speak as if that were nothing, my dear. But no, there was no other objection. Her family's as good as mine. Rather better, actually. With a *dot* it would have been a most advantageous match."

"Well, you earn something from Father, don't you?"

"Which would hardly survive my leaving his daughter, so to speak, on the very steps of the altar!"

"Even with her consent? Even at her suggestion?" I suddenly saw all my problems solved in the exploding brilliance of one noble deed. "Even if I talked Father into accepting it? And look, Oberto. I have a little something of my own which my grandfather left me. It's no great fortune, of course, but it's *something*, and would go further in Italy, wouldn't it? Well, I'll give you half of it as a wedding present! Not now, of course, because Father would stop me, but later, when I'm twenty-one and can do what I like. Oh, Oberto, will you take the chance?"

He seemed very much touched. "Blanche. How could I ever accept anything like that?"

"Very easily. By accepting it."

"No, no, I could never . . ."

"Will you let me talk to Father? Not about the gift part, of course. That would come later. But about our engagement. Can I at least do that?"

"How can I stop you from talking about anything you like in your own family?"

What madness made me think that I could have any effect on my father? I must have clung to the idea that he was really more interested in using Oberto as a tool in his Italian deal than in having him as a son-in-law. I even imagined myself advancing the argument that Oberto, married to his true love, whose social status I rapidly inflated to that of near royalty, would be more valuable to him in the upper echelons of the business world of Milan. And why did Oberto even passively countenance my wild attempt? I suppose because he thought all American fathers and their daughters were just a bit crazy and there was no foretelling what fantastic schemes they might agree upon. At any rate, as he took no part in it, he would have nothing to lose.

I couldn't sleep that night, as I was determined to broach the subject to Father the very next day at breakfast, a meal at which Mother never appeared. Oberto would be present, for he had now, at Mother's invitation, moved from his hotel into a guest chamber on the story above mine. But I wanted him at the table to confirm his willingness to end our engagement.

Stumblingly, awkwardly, I stammered out a sad little outline of my lack of conjugal sentiment and my desire for release. I had to go through it twice, as Father was hardly listening the first time. When he at last took in my meaning, before I had even got to the part about Oberto's other romantic interest, he turned abruptly to the latter, as if he alone needed to be considered in the matter.

"What's this all about, Count? Prewedding flutters? We all know about nervous brides. But can't you take care of it yourself and calm Blanche down so I can enjoy my breakfast in peace?"

"Oh, certainly, sir."

"And by the way, in case you're wondering if Miss Change-her-mind isn't too volatile a consort to grace your ancestral acres, I'm planning to sweeten the pill a bit. I made a lucky sale last week, and I'm instructing my lawyer, in addition to the settlement already made, to draw up a little document in which, starting on the day of your wedding, I agree to pay your wife an annuity of twenty-five hundred dollars!"

"Ah, Mr. Schweizer, that is really princely of you!"

And that was all! Not another word was vouchsafed to my proposal. When I tried to talk to Oberto about it after our meal, when Father had gone to his room to get ready to leave for the office, he simply shrugged his shoulders and raised his eyebrows as if to ask what could he do? The matter, so far as he was concerned, had been taken out of his hands. He then left the house to go downtown with Father.

He had bought me — that was the long and short of it — and bought me for a paltry extra $2500 a year! The duke of Marlborough would have taken the first Cunarder back to England had Consuelo Vanderbilt's father dared even to mention so small a sum. And here was I, Blanche Schweizer, plighted to marry a man weaker than the weakest cat, a man whom it would be impossible now to respect, let alone to love, and whom, if I were really obliged to go through with the ceremony, I should probably come to hate!

Yet when I rushed to Hanky for consolation and advice, it was to receive this horrified protest:

"But, my dear, your wedding is only four days off! I've been helping your mother do the seating of the pews. The presents are all here. And all that linen, all those sheets and towels, all that silver hopelessly monogrammed BSG! Oh, Blanche, think of the scandal! You can't do it, my child! You really can't!"

"Must my life be ruined because of initials on washrags?"

"Washrags! They're on the George III coffee urns your uncle Franz gave you!"

Such were Hanky's ultimate values! I could think only of Juliet's exclamation about her nurse: "Ancient damnation! O, most wicked fiend! . . . Thou and my bosom henceforth shall be twain."

Of course, Hanky had not, like Juliet's nurse, counselled bigamy, and I was ultimately to forgive her, but never again did I place the same reliance on her judgment.

In the tumultuous fury of my mind in the next few days I must have waxed almost irrational. Brooding in my chamber, refusing to come down to meals — Mother gave orders that I was to be left alone until I came to my senses, and allowed trays to be sent up — I at last devised a desperate plan that would not only blow my wedding to pieces but would wreak a terrible revenge on my parents and my betrothed.

My idea grew out of the scene in my favorite novel, *Jane Eyre,* where the heroine's marriage to Mr. Rochester is aborted by the revelation from one of the congregation, in response to the minister's demand if there be any impediment to the rite, that the groom has a living spouse. I had no knowledge of any existing Countess Gulinelli, other than the formidable dowager, but I should provide the impediment myself by crying out to all present that I could neither love nor obey this man!

What would ensue? My expulsion from the church, from my home, from my family? Would I find myself thrown in the gutter in a soiled wedding gown? What did I care? I was half hysterical; I hardly ate, said not a word to a soul, even Hanky. My conduct was ascribed to bridal jitters; nobody was allowed to pay any attention to it. I was living now in the prospect of one glorious moment, one splendid burst of self-expression, a kind of orgasm, as I see it now, a love death or hate death, as in the end of Wagner's great music drama. If *Jane Eyre* was my favorite novel, *Tristan* was my favorite opera.

Frantically, I kept up my resolution until the wedding day, when I presented myself, with apparent meekness, in readiness to be dressed and go through with the ceremony. It was not until I was actually proceeding down the long aisle on my father's arm that reality began to break through. Who, I suddenly asked myself, was the big man so conducting me, so uncomfortably tight and sweating in a new cutaway ordered to measurements that his vanity would not allow to fit his grossness? And who was the overdressed lady with the huge hat in the last pew on my right, dabbing a dry eye in deference to custom as her daughter passed to her doom? And who was the vapid tall dark individual with his vapid tall dark best man waiting for me at the foot of the altar? Were they anything but the honor cards dealt *me* to play *my* hand? If I was to make game I should have to play it in a stronger suit. Well, play it I would!

At last the minister asked, in the hasty, perfunctory tone that some clergymen adopt for a routine seen as faintly embarrassing, if there existed an impediment to the proposed union. My glance darted from Oberto to my father and then, lingeringly, to Mother. All three had their eyes peeled on me with nervous apprehension. They *knew* of my project! Or at least they were waiting, in horrid anticipation, for something they deemed almost, but not quite — oh, no, not quite — impossible. I had them in my grip. I could do with them what I chose!

And so I said nothing. I allowed my little plan to evaporate into the upper air of that high-ceilinged church. But it was a new Blanche who walked back down that aisle as Countess Gulinelli. It was a Blanche who would learn to cope with a weak but essentially compliant husband, with his bossy but manageable old mother, with her own father's ultimate bankruptcy and the loss of her dowry, who would undertake the management of the hitherto ill run Gulinelli farms and eke out a living for her son and daughter and who, as a widow in the Second World War, in the German occupation of northern Italy, aided by her gallant offspring, would provide hidden shelter and conduit for escaped Allied prisoners of war. Even Hanky heroically helped! At eighty-six she was made a dame of the British Empire and died content. *Her* dreams had come true.

The Interlude

1.

THERE WAS NO QUESTION in Angelica Brooks's mind as to
what had altered her life from a freely flowing river to a slug-
gish tidal area losing its force and impetus in soggy marshland.
It was her resignation in 1952, three years before, from the Wall
Street law firm that bore her father's name and of which her
husband, Sidney, was the brightest and most up-and-coming
of the junior partners. She had been just thirty at the time and
an associate in the trust and estates department — admittedly
a minor, almost an "accommodation," section of a corporation
firm — but she had been hoping against hope that her good
record and the changing times might override what was still the
prejudice in the larger houses against making female partners,
when her father had taken her out to lunch to enlighten her. It
had not been an easy thing, for who but he had urged her to go
to law school in the first place? His tone was heavy, and his great
shaggy head had shaken in regretful nods.

"Having a junior partner and an associate who are married to
each other has already been frowned at in the firm," he told her,
"but I have been able to control that. Having two partners who
are mates I might not be able to, let alone the die-hard attitude

of a few old stick-in-the-muds about having a woman partner at all. You may well ask, if that be the case, why I let you come into the firm. The truth is, I thought the training would be valuable for you in whatever you did afterwards, and I assumed that any-one as brilliant and charming as yourself would soon be married and too busy raising a family to bother with our dusty old books and cases downtown."

"Do you imply, Daddy, that I have been neglecting Tim and Elly?"

"In no way, my dear. They're wonderful kids and doing splendidly in nursery school, and I know how conscientiously you spend your nights and weekends with them. Indeed, your mother and I have even worried about the effect on your social life. But the fact remains that here in the office you may be on a dead-end street. As far as partnership goes, that is. You can al-ways command the highest going salary rate for your age as an associate. But I know that's not what you want. Still, you should count your blessings, my precious girl! You have a successful and utterly devoted husband, two great children, no financial worries, plenty of friends and outside interests, a first-class brain and all the charm anyone could ask. Honey, the world's your oyster!"

"What world?"

Sidney was much better about it than her father when he came home late that night. He was working on a hideously tangled corporate reorganization and was pale from his hours of toil, but paleness was becoming to his slightly haggard dark good looks. As always he gave his most serious attention to anything that concerned her.

"I don't want you to stay on, darling, if you can't be a partner, and your father has finally convinced me that we haven't the votes. You could get a job in another firm fast enough, and some of the smaller ones are getting much less stuffy about making woman partners, but I've been wondering if you wouldn't do better to take a year off and think over what you'd really like. Forgive me if I've sometimes doubted your total dedication to the law. I'm not, mind you, in the least questioning your expertise."

"Well, there's a limit, it's true, to my adoration of wills and estates. Sometimes I feel like an undertaker." She felt the least bit depressed, as sometimes happened, at his eternal reasonableness. He was always so fair, so balanced, so devoted. He could never see there were moments when she just wanted to spit in the eye of the world. And she was uncomfortably aware that her own amusement in putting together the jigsaw puzzle of an estate plan that would least benefit Uncle Sam was a pale simulacrum of the "hard, gemlike flame" of his passion for the legal machinery that turned the wheels of industrial competition. The practice of law to Sidney was an art to which everything else came second. Even herself, even the children! But she couldn't complain about that. It had been the thing that had first intrigued her about him.

"I can see you in a lot of other things," he went on. "In politics, for example. You speak so well, and you have a way with people. And you care about causes. How about getting involved with the Democratic party organization?"

He really *was* thinking about what she should best do. Had her father ever, really? Even when he had gone along with her desire to be a lawyer, in his image, hadn't he been flattered by the vision of an adoring daughter, adoring and adored, turning into a kind of lovely Portia? Hadn't it been a fantasy?

Ethan Drury had filled the heaven and earth of her childhood and adolescence. He had been the sky, whether fair or stormy, over the sober, the sometimes God-fearing commuting community of Gulls Cove on Long Island; his small, riveting eyes, sometimes glinting with a kindness almost akin to love, but never missing a slip or a tumble, had penetrated to her boarding school, to Vassar, to Columbia Law, and even in the great gray city where so many of his grinding hours were spent, they swept the narrow dark streets of the financial district and reached to the escape vents of Times Square and the parks. Daddy's power was felt by the family, by his firm, by his great corporate clients and by the Plattsburg camps for officers' training that he had helped to organize in both wars and by the thousands of men who had been conscripted by the draft laws for whose passage he had so passionately and powerfully lobbied. He was male, incorruptibly male, the incarnation of his sex; he believed in war, holy war, and might even have been grateful for the existence of the Hun to keep Mars alive and kicking.

He was appropriately large and heavy and strong with a high brow and bushy gray hair, and although he had a habit of nervous twitches and rather stertorous breathing, his grave stare created an atmosphere of awesome stillness like a chamber of justice in which anything but the truth was unthinkable to tell. Drury represented great companies in their strife, and Angelica was too well educated to be unaware that bad things went on in that strife, yet her father's reputation for honesty and integrity somehow towered over the nefarious doings of his partners and clerks. She sometimes thought of him as a saintly pope presiding over a wily college of Italian cardinals. Was it possible that they kept certain things from him? If so, they had to be inordinately clever.

Angelica had never been jealous of her mother or of her three younger sisters. The latter were giggly, boy-crazy, party-loving, amiable creatures, greedy for the prizes then accorded to their sex and spoiled and coddled by a conventionally doting sire. Their mother played the tart, realistic ("no fancy pants") part of the good plain wife who keeps her seer of a spouse from being lost in the ether of his high thoughts, but this was a veil to cover her almost servile subjection to his every whim and wish. If she was a good-tempered Fricka and the sisters obedient if rather shrill Valkyries, to Angelica was left the function of the best beloved, Brunhilde, the intimate and confidante of Wotan.

But of course Wotan had wanted a son. How could he not? What would he be, in the end, in the twilight, without a Siegmund, a Siegfried? And hadn't he almost had one in the most devoted of clerks, the lean sleek hound ever at his heels with eyes upturned for the least command, Sidney Brooks, his master's right hand, whose subtler and more imaginative mind superbly complemented the older man's and made their joint effort a masterpiece? Sidney had spent his weekends with the Drurys in the big airy shingle mansion in Gulls Cove and when he was not working with Daddy, he was sailing or playing tennis with Angelica. With whom could she more properly fall in love than with Sidney? And with whom could he than with her? Did it really matter that both were in love with her father? And that father, had *he* ever been in love? How could he have been? Let him, like his hero, Theodore Roosevelt, stand at Armageddon and battle for the Lord!

"The world is changing," her father had told her one winter night during the war at their hotel in Washington where he had invited her to accompany him on one of his lobbying missions to the capital. "And the war is bound to speed that up. Your mind, my dear, is too fine not to be trained like a man's. You've been as much help to me in drafting memoranda to this Senate committee as any of the young men from my office. I think you ought to go to law school next year."

She was elated. Wotan had praised her for bringing a dead hero to Valhalla! And the following fall found her enrolled in the first-year class at Columbia Law.

The final seal of paternal approval had been placed on her

in one of her courses. As a distinguished graduate of the law school, her father had been invited to take over a class in criminal law. He had started his own career in the district attorney's office and had never lost his interest in the prosecution of felony. Angelica thrilled with pride as she watched the large, rumpled, grizzled figure of her father amble slowly to the rostrum to address the class.

"Rape!" he exclaimed throatily. "I see rape is the felony on your schedule for today. Well, let us see what we can make of this repellent but persistent vice in our afflicted society. Will someone offer me a definition of rape?" As no one volunteered, he consulted a class list of names and addresses. "Let me call on a gentleman from one of our southern states: Mr. Darlin, of Atlanta. Mr. Darlin, will you favor us with such a definition?"

Mr. Darlin's deep drawl amused the class. "I think I might call it the violation of the chastity of a young lady."

"Well, you've got some pretty good Victorian terms there. And I don't, by any means, wish to knock Victorianism, as many are too prone to do these days. But I'm afraid your definition is subject to the same criticism as Voltaire offered to that of the Holy Roman Empire when he said it was neither holy, nor Roman, nor an empire. Your victim, I must point out, Mr. Darlin, need not be young nor chaste nor a lady, whatever that latter term is construed to mean."

The class roared, and poor Mr. Darlin blushed furiously. Angelica raised her hand, and her father immediately pointed to her.

"It's the penetration by force of a woman's vagina by the penis of a male."

"Very good, Miss Drury!" He did not hesitate to show that he knew her. "Your definition unhappily is not exclusive, as there seem, alas, to be other forms of penetration, but it will do excellently for a start. And tell me, how far must this intruding male organ penetrate?" Here he stretched out his right arm to make it seem the instrument described. "This far?" With his left hand he grasped his wrist. "This far?" He shifted his grasp to his elbow. "This far?" Now he clasped his right shoulder. "Or this far?"

Angelica smiled. "Any amount. The least fraction of an inch will do."

"Right, Miss Drury! Very good! *Any* amount."

And she felt at last the excitement of being on equal terms with him! Together they had bridged the gulf of sex and reticence. However much in the future he orated about the duty of men to kill and of women to bear children, they would have firm ground in common.

2.

As she looked back, retracing the steps of her life which she had once sought to liken to the slow but steady rise of an escalator but which she now found more to resemble a moving beltway crossing a dull level from one drab gateway to another, it seemed to her that that brief moment in the criminal law class had really been the last in which she and her father had been as one. Ever afterwards had she not been gently but very firmly molded to fit the role which he, however much the benevolent father, had deemed, in his greater wisdom, to be the most appropriate one, to be perhaps the *only* one that her circumstances would allow? It must have been clear to so keen an observer of the times as Ethan Drury, to a man who had foreseen wars and victories, that women were not going to accept forever the Rough Rider's concept of the babe-in-arms wife stoically waving her man off to the front lines of carnage. No, modifications had certainly to be made, and who knew better how to make them than such an old gray practitioner at the bar? Women had to be given the *appearance* of lawyers.

And so, on graduation from law school among the highest in her class she had been given a job in the paternal firm, but not as a litigator, which had been her first choice, or in corporation law, her second, but in trusts and estates, her father explaining that it was a good place for a woman to start, as some of the rich female clients might be inclined to favor the advice of their own sex in threading the tortuous path between the impact of estate taxes and the welfare of their nearest and dearest and particularly in confiding any doubts they might have as to the financial capacity or trustworthiness of certain male members of their clan. That it was not the straightest path to partnership was clear — only two of the sacred thirty were in that work — but there was no rule that one had to stay permanently in any one field of the firm's practice, and Angelica had bowed to the wishes of her parent and boss.

And somehow, of course, she *did* remain where she had started, becoming — oh, yes — skilled and respected in the preparation and administration of wills. And then Sidney Brooks returned to the firm after four years of naval sea duty, resuming his place in corporate mergers and reorganizations as her father's right hand, with the halo of an incipient partnership shining on his handsome brow. The weekends at Gulls Cove were resumed and the long Saturday nights working over registration statements with the boss, but so were the tennis and sailing with Angelica. She could not fault Sidney's devotion to the boss's eldest daughter nor attribute it to self-interest, so assured, with or without her aid, was his future in the firm.

Yet it took him a good year to win her. She told her mother, who, of course, favored his suit, that it would be a question of turning herself from Daddy's daughter into Daddy's daughter-in-law. "Sidney is his real child," she would complain, almost with a will to be bitter, and she would liken the pair to a gruff old bear and a lithe, lean hound, incongruously hunting together. And yet there were moments, and rather wonderful ones, when she was almost awed by the single-minded devotion that she seemed to have inspired in this remarkable young man. Her sisters found him romantic and her hesitation idiotic; it was their silly theory that he was Byronic under his unaccountable feeling for anything as dull as the law, that he was aflame beneath his too sober exterior, that he had never been in love before and never would be again.

However grave and quiet and concentrated, he yet took an intelligent interest in many things outside the law. If he embarked on a new field at her suggestion, as with the games of bridge and croquet, he rapidly mastered their techniques. Nor did he ever seem to lose his temper; if something did make him angry, he was very still. He never boasted about his war record, but her father made it clear to everyone that he had earned a Silver Star. It was impossible, in short, not to return some of the love that he so stubbornly yet discreetly offered. How could one *not* marry a man so supremely eligible?

She did and was almost smothered in the congratulations of family and friends. Would it have been better if the course of true love had not flowed quite so smoothly? They were married in Gulls Cove, with the entire firm attending; they settled in the charmingly converted two upper stories of a brownstone on the East Side, with the weekend use of a gardener's cottage on the family place. The right number of children, a boy and a girl, were born in rapid succession, and in due course, as has been seen, Sidney was raised to partnership and Angelica gave up the law to become a full-time wife and mother.

As she had a full-time nurse, however, and a part-time cook, she immediately found that she had time on her hands, and, after a brief but competent survey of the charitable opportunities available, she agreed to join the board of an old and worthy settlement house. "Your being a lawyer, my dear," the director assured her, "will come in so handy." Angelica knew that this would not be true and that the house counsel was quite adequate for any legal problems arising. She perfectly understood that fundraising was the almost sole function of any charitable organization's board, and to fundraising she directed all her skill and imagination.

In the course of only two seasons she made a name for herself as the creative genius of the charity ball. She learned not only who was who in the different spectra of New York society; she learned, even more importantly, which ladies would work on a given task and which would only say they would, and her committees became models of efficiency. She was soon in demand from other charities, hospitals and museums and schools, to act as chairman or co-chairman of one of their annual events. She knew the perils of a bad table seating and how to devise an appetizing but rapidly served dinner; she perfected the art of successfully soliciting free liquor, free decorations and even free music, and she almost put a stop to the stealing of cases of wine by caterers' staff.

Her most valuable ally, and one that she soon used exclusively, even making its retention a condition for her taking on a job, was Posh Inc., a public relations firm that handled anything from a bar mitzvah to a state funeral, and the representative she always asked to work with her was a young man called Chub Perry. He looked indeed even younger than his thirty-odd years; he was diminutive and blond and blue-eyed, with an amiable mild lisp and a gaze of seeming innocence, which had nothing to do with his extreme shrewdness, his wildly inventive imagination and his down-to-earth realism. He was also a scandalmonger of the most salacious type, and he would entrance the committee ladies with whom he worked by interspersing their labors with spicy stories about people they knew or hoped to know and applauding his own wit with oddly infectious screeches of laughter. Angelica's initial distancing of herself from the gossipy side of this new associate was soon overcome by what she could not wholly misread as his sincere admiration. Chub fully appreciated the value of her work, and he seemed to offer what struck her as a more genuine friendship than that which he casually tossed to the other ladies.

She made the mistake of inviting him for dinner one night as a needed extra man at a party for one of her husband's clients. Two of Sidney's slightly older partners and their wives were present: the finest types the firm could offer, she had to admit. The men were of wide, general interests, polite, concise, logical, almost as ready to listen as to talk, certainly so if the speaker was an important, older man and a client. Their wives, who *had* been pretty, and still could have been had they been as cosmetically industrious as the fashionably svelte society types at whom they quite honestly sniffed, verged now ever so slightly on the dowdy but were still serene in their confidence in their happy homes, their civic duties and the fundamental rightness of a world whose inequalities and injustices they were yet too intelligent to underestimate.

And Chub didn't fit in at all, as he clearly saw, poor boy, in the polite chill that followed one of his awful stories. Angelica felt that she might as well have invited an Australian aborigine; indeed, that would have interested them far more. She supposed, miserably, that the table was correct in its judgment of Chub and his anecdotes — if not, what was her whole life but a farce?

Yet if it *was* a farce, didn't she belong up there before the foot-lights on the vaudeville stage, swapping crude jokes with the top banana and not in the dark, unresponding, mirthless pit? She yearned for the curtain to drop.

Afterwards, alone with Sidney, she took the unusual step of pouring herself a stiff nightcap. He watched her without com-ment. He did not join her.

"Of course, you've crossed him off as a fairy," Angelica said.

"A homosexual? I prefer the term to your pejorative one. Should I cross him off for that?"

"Oh, you're always so damn reasonable! I know I can never catch you out in a prejudice. But you despise him just the same."

"I don't despise him at all. It's true that I thought him too free in his stories about clients. I realize that he may not be bound by the same rules of discretion that govern the bar, but even so I couldn't quite —"

"Oh, I know, he's awful," she interrupted impatiently. "He has no business talking out of school like that. Forgive me. I'm tired and cross. I've had a long day."

"Come to bed, dear."

There was no point trying to pick a fight with Sidney; she was bound to lose. But she was more and more uncomfortably aware of the widening rift in her life between her home and her work. The children, four and three, were delightful when they *were* delightful; her father was as benign as ever, if inclined to be a bit sarcastic about her charity balls; and Sidney, of course, so genuinely interested in anything she did, so anxious to help, was sometimes even able to solve a problem that baffled Chub, though his mind, she knew, was always shadowed by his basic preoccupation with some corporate problem. And her own mind, did it not constantly return to the pleasant lunches at fine restaurants that often followed their committee meetings, when the ladies would take Chub along to enliven the meal, and they all would explode with mirth over a particularly nasty story and a second cocktail?

It was as if, having been relegated to a woman's world of the nineteen fifties, she was taking a perverse delight in undermining the one from which she had been ousted, by outraging its shibboleths. The society of women who supported the lavish entertainments that raised the money for charitable causes was opulent and worldly. It was, as Angelica saw it, a society of the wives of the clients, or of the sort of clients, for whom her husband and father toiled. But these women made short shrift of the little idealisms of the downtown bar; they took the money that their husbands made and blew it on clothes and jewels and splendid homes; they *lived* while their men merely existed. Angelica began even to wonder if women were wise to fight for a world where they would wear the same shackles as the other sex. In her fevered fantasies she thought of herself as a triumphant courtesan in ancient Alexandria, Thaïs in her palace of pleasure, and Sidney as the fanatical monk in the desert, Paphnutius, who could only pray that her revels would not spread to engulf his monastery.

The time came soon enough when it was not wholly fantasy.

The committee meeting for the January ball had not been scheduled for the usual conference chamber in the Settlement House, which was being repainted, but, at Chub's suggestion, at his own exquisite *boîte* of an apartment on Bank Street in the Village. And the ladies were delighted to pay a visit to his three high-ceilinged rooms on the *piano nobile* of a Federal-style house, redolent of incense and crammed with *papier-mâché* furniture, scarlet curtains, needlepoint cushions, and vivid photographs of luscious nudes of both sexes. Chub offered them every sort of drink, cheese and cracker; he was the most charming and accommodating of hosts, and when the brief business of the day had been accomplished, the five women stayed on to drink and gossip. All were in an easy and confidential mood; husbands and children and daily cares were laid aside; the world for the moment was reduced to the enchanting irresponsibility of Chub's perfumed interior.

As the hour drew on towards dinnertime the ladies began to take their leave. Chub offered to cook eggs for any who cared to stay, but none availed themselves of his invitation, looking at their watches and exclaiming about their scanted obligations. Angelica, leaning back on the sofa with her third martini, announced suddenly, somewhat to her own surprise, that Sidney was in Washington for a couple of days, that the children were at a birthday party with their nurse, and that she could think of nothing pleasanter than to linger at Chub's for a dish of scrambled eggs.

The ladies were mildly surprised, but no eyebrows were raised. She knew what they all thought of Chub.

"It's a good time for Chub and me to work out the seating for the party," she threw in as an explanatory dividend.

"Oh, if you'll do *that,* my dear . . ." And, pleased to have that chore off their hands, they departed before Angelica could change her mind.

Alone with her host, she told him more about her life and her doubts than she had ever told anyone before, and he listened, charmingly. Then he told her about his own life: how impossible his father was and had always been, sneering at his job, his friends, his apartment, always trying to lure him back into the family insurance business, where he had briefly started and from which he had fled, and how dear his pretty loving little mother was, despite her constant and intrusive silly suggestions and ideas. He went on to tell her of his ambition one day to write a wonderful novel about New York and all the events he had helped to organize, and the jealousies and backbiting he had had to witness. She watched him while he got out the scraps for the beautiful Siamese cat; she broke the eggs into the pan for him to cook; she nodded when he held up for her approval a bottle of champagne. Two glasses on top of the gin she had consumed gave her a dreamy sense of utter freedom from the world beyond the red curtains that he had now pulled, a feeling more delightful and relaxing than anything she could remember having previously experienced.

When he suggested, after their little supper, that they make love, it was as if he were simply offering to crown their evening with a rare old brandy reserved for some special occasion. She was not in the least put off or shocked. She simply smiled.

"So you *do* go in for the girls."

"People take one so for granted," he retorted, with only a mild pique. "They like to stick everyone into cubbyholes. Queer or straight? Which are you? Well, choose, damn you! To me it's all a question of *when*. A man is committing a homosexual or heterosexual act at a particular point of time. Why eternalize it? Am I an alcoholic if I drink a cocktail?" He had moved to the bar table and was indeed now opening an old bottle of brandy, his back to her. It emphasized the casualness of the scene and the occasion. "I'm not going to talk about what I've done or not done in the past. I'm interested in the present. I should be very pleased to make love to you, my dear, and there wouldn't have to be any consequences. There wouldn't even have to be a tomorrow. I have no wish to interfere with that handsome husband of yours or to have anything at all to do with your marriage. But I have an idea that you and I could give each other a very nice time tonight. *If* we both wanted to."

The fact that he made no offer to touch her, to embrace her, even to approach her, she found very attractive. The bottle he was opening struck her as a proffered, civilized alternative to what she might decide to decline. When he turned to her, he was smiling, but it was a serious smile. He wished to be accepted precisely on his terms or not at all. He seemed suddenly more mature, more — she was almost ashamed to observe it — of a man.

"Give me some brandy," she said.

When she had sipped it, she felt a delicious humming in her head. Everything he had said seemed entirely logical and true. He was *not* interfering with anything in her life unless she chose to see it so.

"Chub, dear, will you turn off the lights?"

"Puritan! You shut God out so He won't see us. But neither will you see the ivory skin of which I'm so proud."

"Do as you're told, dear boy. It's not God I'm shutting out. I want to be in Never-Never Land."

He chuckled as he went to the switch. "How true. It's Peter Pan you want. Very well. Peter Pan you'll have."

It was like nothing that had ever happened to her. It was all very well to say it was natural, but it *was* natural, natural and easy as it had never quite been for her before. It had nothing to do with Sidney, or with the children, or even with Daddy; and it flashed across her mind that Sidney would be wrong to be jealous. She had an absurd vision of a large marble group she had seen in some museum, a sugary Victorian concept of the babes in the woods, sleeping enclasped in each other's arms on the floor of the forest primeval.

Chub's tact did not end with their union. Afterwards, as they dressed, he was silent, not speaking until he insisted on seeing her home in a taxi. At her house he waited to be sure she had her key; he didn't get out.

"Remember, my dear" began his last words of the evening. "When you wake up in the morning, you may have a slight hangover. But that is all. Last night? It didn't happen. Because it didn't have to."

It was kind of him, very kind. But it wasn't true. It *had* happened.

Sidney was still in Washington, so she was alone in her bedroom when she awakened the next morning. Chub had been quite right; she *did* have a hangover. It was only to have been expected that she should be thinking about him, but she was surprised that her train of thought should be so free of emotion. She certainly did not "love" her last night's lover; she did not even feel a wish to repeat the experience. It was something that had happened to her, all right, but it was a happening that did not seem to have any necessary relation to the rest of her life; it was as if she had taken an unexpected spin into space on a rocket and landed back in the ocean with a surprisingly small splash. And no one had noticed that she had left.

The same mood continued in the following week. Sidney returned and did not seem to see any change in her. The children were just as dear, just as cheerful, just as trying. And at the next meeting of her committee, in the now repainted conference chamber of the Settlement House, Chub's behavior was perfect. He called her "darling" and "my dear" as he did the other ladies, but without the slightest change of inflection, nor did he once try to catch her eye, or seek, after the meeting, to have a word with her alone. He might have sensed what was going on in her mind and wished to leave her the full liberty of working it out. Or he might have simply thought it wiser to stay clear of any possible emotional involvement. Who knows, he might have asked himself, what strange storms may wrack the heart of a suddenly awakened woman in her thirties? Had such not been known to reach for a gun?

But Angelica knew that he was quite safe. Whatever storm

was coming — and she was pretty sure that one was on the way — there would be no danger of violence. She understood now that Chub was only a minor player in her drama, that what she had *done* with him was everything, that he himself was the smallest part of it. It was not that he would be killed and eaten after copulation, as in the case of some male insects; he could get away and play his role, exactly as before, in the party planning part of her charitable work. What she had to face was what she had done to herself: she was now a woman who had hardly hesitated to place an act of the grossest carnal delight in the very center of the broad fair avenue of her spousal, maternal and filial duties.

And had she not justified every precaution the other sex had taken through the ages to put bars between the woman and her lust: the convents in which European fathers had locked up their teenage daughters, the chaperons so rigidly required on all occasions where the sexes mingled, the flowing robes and veils in which Eastern men smothered their women?

But that was not what was now most haunting her, growing rapidly to a near obsession. It was not the folly of men in not allowing women to be just as they were; it was the fact that she was no longer the person that the men and women of her acquaintance thought her. At dinner parties now with her husband's and father's partners and clients, and, of course, their presumably virtuous spouses, she would always be faced with the idea of how very differently they might judge her should there loom in their minds a picture of her rolling naked on a divan in the company of a naked pansy, fairy, faggot — or whatever they had the malice to dub him — and crying out, squealing, with pleasure!

Or was she exaggerating their reactions? Wasn't there a dirty side to even the cleanest of minds? And who knew, who really knew, what they themselves had been up to? But even if she could dismiss them and what they might be thinking — and she thought that in time she might — how could she live with a wrong image of herself in the minds of the two men around whom she had built her life?

And she decided at last that she could not.

3.

She had selected, following their lunch, her father's office as the stage for the little drama that might, she feared, have smacked a bit of masochism. Was it like shouting heresy before the altar of a cathedral? But it was certainly a sober side of her project to place the confrontation of her acts and her supposed ideals in the inner sanctum of the philosophy of life that she had most cultivated. The room was large, oblong and paneled, with scant heavy mahogany furniture and old prints of British judges. The great table desk in one corner was clear of ornaments and papers except for a neatly stacked little pile of the latter in the center of the blotter which would presumably become the object of the occupant's burning attention as soon as she had departed.

"Very well," her father told her, glancing at his watch, "I am all ready for your 'confession.'" He allowed himself a wink to show how little he expected anything really bad. "I can give you twenty minutes."

"I shall need no more than five. Let me put it right on the carpet. I have committed an act of adultery."

The full extent of his shock was evident in the quick drop of his jaw and the way his hands rose from the desk as if to ward off anything further. His eyes would not meet hers. He looked away.

"*One* act?" Oh, the lawyer! How quickly he reached for an extenuation.

"I suppose you'd call it one. There was a single meeting."

"And do you intend to repeat it?"

"No. I don't think I do."

"Who knows about this?"

"The partner to it. The young man I've been working with at the Settlement House. And now you."

"Not Sidney?"

"No, he doesn't dream it."

"Then, my dear, it doesn't exist!" He rose now and walked to a window, his broad back somehow defiantly confronting her.

"But it *does* exist, Daddy. Because it's a part of me. And now I want it to be a part of *you*. And I have every intention of making it a part of Sidney."

"Even if he divorces you?" He did not turn.

"Even so. But I don't think he will."

At this he did turn, his eyes burning with exasperation. "In God's name, *why,* Angelica, must you inflict this on us? Why can't you make your own silent atonement for what you have so inexplicably and uncharacteristically done and let us all go on about our business in peace?"

"Because what I did was neither inexplicable nor uncharacteristic. It was *me*, Daddy, part of a real me, and I want the two men who have been my mainstay to know it!"

"They'll be more your mainstay if you keep it to yourself!"

"Daddy, you're not helping me!"

"I'm trying to! How can you dignify one moment of aberration, a solitary instance, something which you don't even wish to repeat, by making it an integral part of yourself? It's as if . . ." Here he turned back to the window. "As if — pardon my language — you'd made a vulgar noise, all right, broken wind, in a room by yourself, and no one was there to hear it. Like the proverbial tree falling in the lonely forest. Was there a noise?"

"I don't like your image at all. But I guess I was afraid that you *would* see it that way. It's been a part of my world that you always might see it that way. Anyway, it helps me now to see that we must see things — certain things at least — differently."

At this he returned to his desk. She was shocked by the pain in the face before her. "How do *you* see the thing you say is a part of you? As a part you approve of? As something that's part of a marriage? Part of a good and decent and lasting marriage, as yours, in my perhaps too sentimental view, has always been?"

"It has nothing to do with my marriage. It has to do with me."

"And you used to call me a puritan! Could anything be more innately Protestant, more Calvinistic? Maybe we should never have left Rome. Our Catholic friends at least have that advantage over us. They can always blame the devil at work in them and not themselves. And the devil is always there, in everyone, so they needn't feel especially heinous. Confess, and you're pure again! Become a Catholic, if you like, my girl. Anything to get this absurd, this ridiculous, this *irrelevant* thing off your too tender conscience!"

How he grasped for a theory! The lawyer again, always, reaching for the question that will stump the suddenly difficult, the oddly recalcitrant witness. She rose to go.

"And so I might even become Daddy's girl again."

"You've never not been, baby."

"Perhaps that's been my trouble."

With that she left. He knew her too well to protest further.

When Sidney came home that night at the unusually early hour of six and greeted her with a novel gravity, she knew that something had happened. Without even going to their room to wash, he went straight to the bar table in the living room and mixed two cocktails. Silently, he handed her one and they both sat down.

"Your father has told me. He thought I had to be prepared. He was afraid I might do something stupid or violent."

As she stared into his grave unblinking eyes and took in the oddly relaxed rigidity of his pale features, she wondered in a strange blank moment if she had ever really known this man.

"Father judged you by himself," she said.

"I don't think he judged me at all. He was too upset."

"Well, he certainly judged *me*. I was in little doubt of that. And how about you, Sidney? Do *you* judge me?"

"Oh, Angelica. I only seek to understand you. Of course, I got hot under the collar when your father told me. Would you have wanted me not to?"

She paused, half in surprise. "No, I suppose not."

"And do you know what my second reaction was? I wanted to make a date with that little bastard. I wanted to get him drunk and drag him back to his scented flat and bugger the hell out of him!"

"Sidney!" She was aghast. "You wanted to do *that*!"

"I wanted to do what you had done! I wanted to be in *your* boat. I wanted there to be nothing I could hold against you! I wanted us to be together in sin or lust or whatever damned or damnable thing *you* choose to call it!"

As she continued to stare at this man whom she indeed had not known before, she had the flash of a view of herself, like her father, groping for a rebuttal. A lawyer herself now, she was losing the oral argument. But who, she wondered, with an odd ruefulness, could win against such an opponent as *this*?

"Oh, Sidney" was all she could mutter.

"The important thing is that we do something about your life. I've been aware of that for quite some time now, only I hadn't come up with the right alternative. But only yesterday, lunching with Ralph Parsons of CBS, I learned of a spot in news analysis that might interest you. It involved . . ."

As he talked on, concisely, interestingly, sympathetically, Chub and his scented (she had forgotten she had told him *that*) flat and the feverish excitement of their encounter faded away before the cool and specific items of career alternatives. She knew that Sidney would never so much as by a hint refer again to her and Chub. No, not even to gain a point in the most violent of domestic quarrels — in the unlikely hypothesis of there being any. The sea of life lay before her, glittering but calm. With something like a sigh she took in the bountiful extent of her blessings. She had better start swimming.

The Anniversary

To ME the county of Westchester is the most beautiful of all the counties of the state of New York. I know how many voices would be raised in protest at such a view, playing up the dramatic wilderness of the Catskills and the Adirondacks, or the lovely green stretches of Lake Erie's coastline, but I prefer the more civilized, the delicately ordered and bordered, residential estates of Westchester, with its rolling acres of modestly wooded hills and pleasant verdant valleys. Of course, I realize that much of the countryside has been preserved from the multitudes of the great metropolis to our south by rigid zoning, and perhaps it ill becomes a man of the cloth to over-relish his immunity from a too promiscuous herding of the human flock, but if I start to count my immunities in this globe of starvation and terror, where will I end?

How many Episcopalian clergymen, for example, in all our nation, enjoy the comfort of so large and luxurious a rectory as mine — a near mansion, almost — or the aesthetic delight of the most beautiful of Ralph Adams Cram's Gothic churches, or the social amenities of so welcoming and hospitable an affluent parish? I can say in my defense that I have served my Lord in much humbler surroundings, and that my call to the South Bedford Church came in no way from my instigation, and that, as my wife points out, the rich have souls as well as the poor. But it is still true that I am enjoying the material advantages of my present post rather more fully than a minister should. Oh, yes, I must face that. And I must also face the more insidious danger of a smug satisfaction at my own courage in facing it. Let this journal be my conscience!

All of which is the start of the weekly entry dated September 10, 1961. Does it give me, as is the great purpose of the journal, an idea for tomorrow's sermon? I think not. My considerable (could I call it great?) reputation as a preacher would not long survive a tendency to wax too personal. Episcopalians stem, after all, from the Church of England, and we Anglo-Saxons distrust — with good reason, I impenitently think — the sloppiness of personal revelation. I never need worry too much about sermon topics. I can always use an old one — I am a magpie at keeping things — and there are even those who think my earliest ones were my best. Ah, why is that, why is that? So I can pause here and look out the window over my green lawn and the still leafy woods and the tops of the distant blue hills just visible in an opening I had cut, and enjoy being alive at fifty-six and in the best of health and knowing that tomorrow I shall face a full church and an approving congregation. And that some of the latter may even have forsaken the golf course to bring their worldly houseguests to hear the golden words of the renowned Canon Truesdale!

There, dear Lord, have I sufficiently exposed my vanity?

But He *knows* all that. Just as He knows that I am not really thinking of my sermon. He knows, as He must always know, my innermost fears and doubts. Even when I doubt *Him*! For I have those moments, yes, alas, more and more of them! Didn't He himself? Didn't He voice despair on the cross? My mind is seething with the problem of how to deal with the dinner party that the parish is giving for me and Lally next Saturday night to celebrate our twenty-fifth wedding anniversary.

We shall be toasted by many of the leaders of the community, and I will be expected to respond. How could it be otherwise? And every man and woman in that chamber will be thinking, if I have the presumption to speak of two and a half decades of marital bliss, how I account to myself, in the deep recesses of my tumbled thoughts, for the gap in my orated number of five dark years — from our ninth anniversary to our fourteenth — when Lally was not with me. Not with me! When Lally had eloped, *bolted, run off with,* Eustace Brokaw, abandoning me and our small son and daughter for a life of flesh and sin!

I look at the words I have written and feel the tingling glow of resentment and wrath as if the intervening years had evaporated, and I had never forgiven or forgot. Good God, is it all still there, inside me? Is there no way to wash out the wickedness of abiding hate? Even when I love the wonderful woman who has made my life so good a thing for the last eleven years?

And does it make it worse if I have never shown, by so much as a chewed lip or darkened brow, that the ashes of my old humiliation are still smoldering? That I have convinced my family, friends, parishioners, and even my too sympathizing and vengeful old mother, that I harbor no grudge, that the past has been washed clean off my doorstep where, indeed, the welcome mat was never removed? Was there a subtle hypocrisy in my not having taken a single legal step to establish a separation, let alone a divorce? Or did people say that if I so easily took back the prodigal wife when she so unexpectedly and unrepentantly reappeared to resume quietly her old duties as a spouse and mother, that I couldn't have been *that* much stricken by her desertion? That, after all, I must be a pretty cold fish? Or, worse, that I took her back because I sorely needed her strong support as a minister's consort, which the subsequent dramatic rise of my fortunes as a preacher and clergyman has demonstrated?

And I suppose I must face another aspect of this whole sorry business of my continued agitation and dismay. Has the amount of control that I must have had to exert over my nature in the past eleven years to maintain my attitude of serene beatitude actually nurtured my stifled anger and outrage? I was recently much struck in rereading my favorite of James's novels, *The Golden Bowl,* by the passage where Maggie, the wronged wife, pictures her repressed rage of jealousy as "a wild eastern caravan, looming into view with crude colours in the sun, fierce pipes in the air, high spears against the sky, all a thrill, a natural joy to mingle with, but turning off short before it reached her and plunging into other defiles."

The sudden exultation that James's metaphor excited in me may well be evidence of the violence I have done to myself.

Which may give me at last an idea for my sermon: the importance of one who has suffered a wrong not only to forgive it, but to forgive it articulately, rather than simply behaving as if no wrong had been inflicted. "Father, forgive them; they know not what they do." But supposing they know very well what they do? Should this not be stated, made clear? And should they not — ah, here's the rub; I knew it *had* to be coming — at the same time be given the opportunity to defend, or at least to explain, what they had done and why they had done it? Did I not play a role in the swerve of Lally's heart — or even soul — from myself to Eustace Brokaw? Face it, Titus! If you dare to call yourself a minister of the gospel!

Very well. I'll write it out.

When we were married I was thirty and Lally only twenty-one. After four years in a Boston church, I accepted a call from a small parish on Mount Desert Island in Maine, not in a fashionable quarter of that very fashionable resort, but in a village in the southwestern area, whose church, however, was amply attended in the warm months by members of the summer colony of nearby Northeast and Seal Harbors who preferred our devout and simple service to the dressier ceremonies of the larger Episcopalian temples.

I had been attracted to the position because of the opportunity it offered me to do some serious writing. In the long dark winters when my work was light, when the summer crowd and their multitudinous suppliers and hangers-on had disappeared and the shops had closed, I could take long walks on the rocky shoreline and gaze at the gray sea and the screeching gulls and contemplate the chapter in process of my exegesis of the Gospel of Saint Luke and the Acts of the Apostles, both the work of one hand and that of the man I liked to think of as the first great novelist of the Western world. An historical novelist, I hastily add; a clergyman can hardly imply that he made anything up. Lally was busy, I assumed, with our housework and the total care of two small children. It was bliss — for me. I actually believed that in those five Maine years I had attained the perfect fusion of my churchly duties, my domestic obligations and my worldly ambitions. For I had worldly ambitions — oh, yes, I did. I had no idea of remaining forever in that obscure northern clime. My writing and my talent as a preacher were to bring me to the notice of the great world. Ambition was to be forgiven if it was dedicated to God.

Unhappily, as events were to bring out, our life did not offer the same outlets or satisfactions to Lally. She found the winters cold and lonely, and the occasional company of the "natives," as the summer people called the permanent residents of the isle, dull and gossipy. She was always gracious to them, however, and she never complained to me about the strictures of her life, but I should have taken note that her silences — she had always been on the quiet side — were increasing. And that when I sometimes talked to her about my book in the evenings she wasn't always listening.

And then came the summer when Mrs. Brokaw, a stylish matron from Northeast Harbor, took to attending my Sunday service, and on one fatal occasion brought her son Eustace, not a young man religiously inclined but who could occasionally, particularly when in financial straits, be brought to heel by his despotic mama. Mrs. Brokaw always waited for me on the steps of the church after a service to comment, in her rather florid sincerity, on my sermon, and on this particular day, when my discourse had been on the parable of the laborers in the vineyard, and why they had received the same wage for differing hours of work, God's love being indivisible, our discussion had lasted for some little time. I never cared to interrupt her, even when others were waiting, as I hoped to induce her to contribute substantially, if not in whole, to a much needed new roof on our little church. It was during this discussion, while Mrs. Brokaw was protesting the unfairness to the longer employed laborers, that her handsome and worthless son, glorious in white flannels and a red blazer, was carrying on a flirty chat with my wife. I had thought Lally was despising him. Evidently she was not.

From then on Eustace attended his mother regularly on her Sunday-morning appearances at our church. Lally and I were invited twice to dinner parties at the Brokaws' great shingle mansion in Northeast Harbor, invitations that I accepted eagerly in anticipation of our hostess's future beneficence. I was too much concerned with cultivating Mrs. Brokaw to more than casually note my wife's silent but still noticeable acceptance of her son's vulgar amiability. I even tried to turn the matter into a joke, likening, on our way home from the Brokaws one evening, the three of us to the trio in *Tess of the D'Urbervilles*: Eustace as Alec, Lally as Tess, and myself as Angel Clare.

"Angel Clare," repeated Lally, who so far had not said a

word. "It sounds like a dessert." And she offered no further comment.

Came the day when she went off with him. Without a word or a note to me or a parting kiss for the children. Without even most of her clothes or any of her few little jewels.

Brokaw had taken her to Italy, where they lived for a year in Sicily before he abandoned her. She then went to Rome, where she worked in a travel agency, never once communicating with me, for four inexplicable years. Do I understand her, even to this day? Mama Brokaw, in an awesome fit of apology, virtually rebuilt my little church, and used her considerable influence in ecclesiastical circles to get me reappointed to a modest parish in Long Island, far from the scene of my shameful treatment by her son. There I toiled to rebuild my shattered career with some degree of success. My book was published and enjoyed a gratifying sale and even more gratifying reviews; my preaching brought me invitations to speak at other parishes, but, as our bishop once confided in me, my peculiar matrimonial status was a distinct bar to the advancement that I might otherwise have expected.

Which I must admit was one reason that I gave careful consideration to the offer made in a letter from Lally that arrived out of the blue one morning. She had returned to New York for her father's funeral and was ready, she wrote, to stay, if I was willing to take her back. Her explanation of the past was of the briefest.

"You have always taken comfort in literary comparisons, so I offer you this one. Hamlet feared the devil might be preying on his weakness and his melancholy, 'as he is very potent with such spirits.' All I can say is that summer in Maine I was both weak and melancholy. I was attracted to a worthless man whom I knew to be worthless, and I went off with him in a kind of suicide. Four years of a chaste life have convinced me that nothing like that will happen to me again. But I shall quite understand if you cannot believe that."

I answered her letter, committing myself only to an interview, and a day later she appeared in my study in the parish house.

She had certainly not been punished physically by her sin. My anguished heart took in the bitter fact that she was even lovelier. There were some streaks of premature gray in her blond hair, but they conveyed a sense of greater depth of character, a sense confirmed by the sad serenity of her opaline eyes and a couple of extra lines below her cheekbones. She had said I was prone to literary comparisons, and I half-irritably asked myself if she was going to put *me* in the wrong, as the returning and unapologizing Helen of Troy does to Menelaus in John Erskine's famous tale. How else could his novel have been written? How else could mine?

She seated herself before my desk, apparently at her ease. She even placed her handbag on it and then settled back in her chair.

"Well, Titus, you have read my proposition. I am ready to resume my place as a minister's wife and a mother. I should not expect any exuberant welcome. Our relationship could be as formal or informal as you wish to make it. But I would promise to honor and obey you. Love, where both you and the children are concerned, would have to be earned by all of us. I understand that the situation would not be an easy one. All I can say is that I would do my best to make it work."

If it were going to be a game between us, a contest, that is, of apparent magnanimities, I still held a high trump. "You would be resuming a place I never felt you had vacated," I pointed out. "When I pledged you my troth, it was for my lifetime."

She seemed to be seeking for something behind this. And wasn't there? If what I said was true, why hadn't I accepted her offer the moment it was made? "Was that why you took no steps to divorce me?"

"I do not believe in divorce."

"Then it's agreed? I'm to come back?"

Had I wanted it to be quite this quick? But there I was. What else could I say? "Everything will be as before."

"You mean we will share a bedroom?"

"If you wish."

She paused. "Perhaps not quite at the beginning."

I just repressed a smile. No, the big scene was not going to be entirely hers. "That will be up to you. At home, in the house, I shall treat you just as before. Of course, I can speak only for myself. The children you may find more difficult. But I daresay you'll manage it."

"I can only try."

I said nothing to this, and she glanced about the room as if seeking a clue as to what next to discuss. "Is that all, then? When shall I come?"

"Today, if you wish."

She rose. "Let's say Monday. I think we both need a little preparation. I had not expected that we should come so rapidly to terms. But I guess it's better this way. We may as well get right on with it." She turned to the door and then back to me. "Have you *no* other comment, Titus?"

"What would you have me say?"

"Oh, that you're glad to have me back. Or sorry. That you still have a rag of affection left for me. Or that you don't. That you hate my guts! Anything! Something for me to go on."

"I have nothing to add, Lally."

She smiled, as if to tell me that now she had all she needed. "I see that the children aren't going to be the hardest part!"

Nor were they. Harry was duck soup with her. He and his sister, thirteen and twelve, had promised me that they would be polite to a returning mother whose absence their unforgiving paternal grandmother, despite my injunctions, had secretly coached them to resent, but I suspected — quite rightly, as it turned out — that behind my back they had formed a pact to confine themselves to frigid good manners. However, that had to be Lally's problem. Her behavior, I soon saw, was perfect. When they met she made no attempt to kiss or embrace them. She faced them with a small friendly smile and addressed them clearly and calmly.

"Your father has allowed me to come back on a kind of trial. You will both have the chance to look me over and decide what you think of me before I exercise any kind of parental authority. That I shan't do until we all three agree that the time has come. Until then it will be your father who is entirely in charge. I will simply hope that you treat me with the same courtesy that you would a houseguest, say, a visiting aunt."

If Harry and Hattie were surprised at her mildness and reasonableness — and I think they were — they did not show it. At meals, in those first weeks of our reunion, Lally and I conversed, in rather stilted tones, about the weather, current events and plans for the day. The children addressed their few remarks to me.

Then, one Saturday morning, when I was at the parish house and the children at home, Lally went to the garage to take our car to the village to shop and found one of the tires flat. She returned to the house to ask Harry if he would change it for her. Without a word he promptly and efficiently did so. In thanking him she apparently simply said this:

"I don't suppose there's any job I can do for you as well as you've done this one. But if there is, just call on me."

The following night, when Lally and I were reading in the parlor, Harry came down from his room to consult me, as he often did, on his homework for school. He was desperately looking for a subject for his weekly theme. I had been watching Lally's quiet tactics with the children, and I saw my chance now to give her a hand and alleviate the tenseness of the home atmosphere which was beginning to get on my nerves.

"Why don't you ask your mother? She used in the old days to give me some good tips for my sermons."

Harry hesitated but at last went to her, and they left the room together for a private conference. A week later he got an A for a composition about a boy on an African safari who had changed the tire on his jeep just in time before the dangerous rogue elephant he had been seeking to kill found *him*.

"I didn't write a word of it," Lally assured me when I protested. "I got it all out of him by asking questions."

"Leading questions, no doubt."

"Well, we weren't in a court of law."

When Harry wanted to thank her, she said: "Just give me a peck of a kiss on the forehead." She lowered her head, and he hugged her. Harry was won.

Hattie, of course, belonging to the stronger sex, was harder. One night at family supper she related to me the story of a girl in her class at school whose mother had left her father for another man. She spoke in a high censorious tone, never once glancing in her mother's direction.

"Of course, her mother's a bad, bad woman," she concluded.

I told her sharply that I didn't want to hear another word about it, and Hattie remained sullenly silent for the rest of our uneasy meal. Afterwards I retired to my study, and it was only through Harry that I learned what ensued.

Lally had addressed herself gravely but not reproachfully to her daughter.

"I want you to know, Hattie, that the reason I did not wince when you described your friend's mother as a bad woman was not because I was not hurt. I knew that jab was meant for me, and you can be sure it found its mark. I was very much hurt. But I know how it pains your father if I wince — he is very sensitive — and I have had to control my reactions. You are not the only person who has thrown my past at me. One learns to bear such things. But please try, Hattie, to spare your father in the future. When you and I are alone together you can call me anything you want."

When at the end of two months Lally announced at breakfast that she was giving up the struggle with Hattie and would be leaving us, it was Hattie who, in a flood of tears, flung her arms around her and begged her, successfully, to stay.

After the first year of our reunion, when the church fathers had been convinced that it was working, I received my call from the South Bedford parish, and my career ever since has been one of continual success. Lally has been beyond praise; beloved by our parishioners, indefatigable in her committee work, her neighborhood calls, her hospital visits and in organizing the social events at the rectory. She has been a gracious hostess to visiting clerics and, most importantly of all, a devoted mother and a sympathetic spouse. For ten of the last eleven years we have, as in the first five of our marriage, shared a bedroom. As one of the elders of our church only half-jokingly told me the other day: "If you become Bishop Truesdale, Titus, as we all expect, you'll owe half of it to Lally."

The only thing that has bothered me in our relationship, at least until the doubt that has assailed me today, has been that Lally never loses her temper at me, never shows the natural impatience that any spouse — and mine in particular — is bound on some occasion to feel. That has to be deliberate, doesn't it?

It is obvious that I am getting nowhere with my sermon. I shall certainly be constrained to use an old one tomorrow.

And I still have not decided whether I can state at the anniversary party: "Bless you, my dear, for a quarter century of happiness!"

September 17, 1961. Well, it's over. The party has been and gone. And I certainly provided something of a shock to all those present, including our two children, who came home from their medical and law schools to attend. Lally's reaction, as might have been expected, was the most unexpected. She jumped to her feet when I had finished my little speech and cried out: "Thank you, dear Titus!"

I had not known just how I should end that little speech until I actually ended it. My opening remarks had been benign and banal, the kind expected on such an occasion when a too florid oratory or a too witty cleverness may be deemed a bit to impugn the deep and supposedly unchallengeable sincerity of the speaker. Yet as I spoke — as I heard my own voice, hollow and far away, not at all as I did when I delivered a sermon — I had the distinct impression that everyone in that large chamber was reducing in his or her mind the twenty-five years of our marriage by the five of Lally's absence from our hearth and wondering if I would dare to refer to that gap, and, if I did, how I would still manage to preserve the congenial feeling of the occasion.

And then, in ending, I turned to Lally and raised my glass of champagne. "I want to thank you, my dear, from the bottom of my heart, for eleven years of perfect bliss!"

What a disciplined crowd it was! Hardly an eyebrow was raised. Lally's enthusiastic response was received with smiles and exclamations of pleasure. Further toasts were offered, and in the bidding of good nights at our host's doorway an hour later not a soul indicated by so much as a twinkle or a frown that any exception had been taken to my perhaps too meticulous calculation of the period of my marital bliss. Nor did Harry or Harriet, even when we had all returned to the rectory and dispersed to our respective rooms. The only unusual thing that happened was that Lally lingered behind when I went upstairs and reap-

peared in our chamber a few minutes later with a small tray, a
bottle of bourbon, two tumblers and some ice.

"Really, my dear," I remonstrated, "haven't we had enough to
drink?"

"Just one apiece." She poured me a stiff one and another for
herself. "For the road, as they say. The new road we've taken
tonight. At long last!"

"Lally, I hurt you! I'm so sorry. I don't know what came over
me. Can you ever forgive me?"

"There's nothing to forgive, Titus. Don't be absurd. You've
wanted for years to let people know just how rottenly I treated
you when I ran off with Brokaw. You've watched me worm-
ing my way back into everyone's affection and respect. You saw
that people were beginning to forget that you had ever been
wronged at all. That they were giving you no credit for your
generosity in taking me back. That they might even be saying
you were lucky to have me! Well, thank God you got it out! Or
some of it, anyway. For I'm sure there's more. But the point is
that now you and I can work on it together!"

I sat down suddenly on the side of the bed, weak with relief.
What had I ever done to deserve a wife of this calibre?

"What can I do to start?" I gasped. "What can I do to show
you I'll be a new man?"

"Go and get the children in here before they go to sleep. Get
two more glasses. And then tell them what we've just said to
each other! We'll all drink to it!"

"Oh, not that!" I groaned in dismay.

But I did exactly what she suggested. And I knew that I was
going to continue to do so.

Man of the Renaissance

I T W A S just two years ago, shortly before the start of the war in 1914, that my son, Hugh, died, and my own life seemed to close. He was so full of vigor and spirit and hope that I could never quite repress, for all its cloying sentimentality so alien to my usual tastes, the vision of Daniel Chester French's bas-relief of the beautiful young sculptor, interrupted in his work by death, the hand holding that raised chisel being stayed by that of the skeletal reaper. I had hoped to persuade George Santayana to write a biographical preface to the memorial volume of Hugh's poems that I was preparing on vellum. Hugh had been one of Santayana's favored students at Harvard, but the great philosopher had declined the task, shaking his head sadly and saying: "Ah, my dear Mr. Trevor, it is too painful to write of what that wonderful young man might have accomplished."

I had my volume printed with only my own brief sketch of the poet's life. It had to be brief and simple because every time I was tempted to use a superlative, my mind's eye would catch a glimpse of those laughing dark eyes, and my inner ear would hear the cheerful but derisive "Quit it, Daddy, will you?" But now that this hideous carnage is raging in Europe, and Kaiser Willie, a bloated baby in a steel hat, is trying to impress his dull cousins in London and Moscow that he can be a second Genghis

Khan, the time has come for me to pen a proper memorial to my son and heed no further the imagined protests of the dear departed. For we are living once more in an age of heroes of which number he would surely have been one. If any element of his brave spirit survives, I am sure it is in Flanders breathing what fire and force it can into the Tommies and poilus in the trenches there. Hugh would never have waited for his country to join the fray; he would have hied himself to Canada or Britain to enlist under the Union Jack, and he would have been happy, horribly happy!

Unfortunately, there has to be a good deal of me in this memoir. I can't get around that. Hugh was an only child, and he had the misfortune to lose his adored and adoring mother when he was only nine. An inconsolable widower, I never remarried, and the boy grew up with me, as close as a son and father can be. We shared each other's confidences; we even shared each other's friends; and with that my reader will surely understand that there have been those who have not hesitated to imply that such solidarity between parent and offspring is not a healthy thing and that I may even have constituted the evil genius in Hugh's life. And I have little doubt, furthermore, that my daughter-in-law, for all her tact and good manners, is one of these.

When Hugh married Vivian, I thought I had made every effort not to intrude on their wedded bliss, but I fear that nothing short of my total eclipse or demise would have satisfied her. The American wife has usually little enough trouble accommodating herself to her husband's father, but that is because he rarely constitutes much of a threat to her. He can be kissed, coddled, called "an old darling" and dismissed. It is with her mother-in-law that she must contend for possession of her spouse, and the struggle is often a bloody one. In me, of course, Vivian had to face *both* parents of Hugh, and, beautiful and bright and universally admired as she was and is, she made it clear from the beginning — though she was never so vulgar as to articulate it — that any relationship between us would at best bear the marks of a smiling truce. What was her basic complaint? I think it was that I had spoiled my child. Spoiled him for her? Oh, no, she found him adorable. Spoiled him, I think, for life, for ordinary life. It may have been her notion that I had raised him to believe he was not like other men.

If this were true, even she, I suppose, would not contend it was *all* my fault. There was always the money. People are quick to blame the money, particularly if they haven't much of it themselves. The money, however, did not come from me. Almost all of it was my wife's, and her will divided it equally between Hugh and myself, though I have always regarded my share as held in a moral trust for him. And let me say at once that Hugh never seemed to have any problem with his money. He never blew it on wine or women, or gambled it away in Monte Carlo, or invested it in the crazy ventures of silly young friends; he purchased sound securities, lived well within his income and made wise and generous gifts to charity. He had even at his death put together a superb collection of Italian Renaissance master drawings. Could any man do more? But people are not so easily put off; they are tireless in their quest for the contamination of a fat purse. So it behooves me to go at greater length than I should wish into the financial background of my and my wife's families.

My parents were not rich, but they were certainly not poor, at least in the Rome of the eighteen fifties and sixties, where I was born and raised (I could never be president of the United States) and where American expatriates could live like princes in the leased *piano nobiles* of vast palazzos on an income (ours was derived from a few tenements in lower Manhattan) that would have commanded only the simplest brownstone at home. My father was a painter of picturesque classical landscapes and peasant girls carrying pitchers on their head (one of his studies of the Forum is now in the cellar of the Metropolitan Museum); he knew William Wetmore Story and the Brownings and *tutti quanti*. As a pretty, fair-haired child, playing in the gardens of the Vatican, I attracted the notice of the benign Pio Nono himself, out for a noontime stroll, but when he asked one of his entourage to inquire as to my name, and my good Protestant American nurse had stoutly replied, "*Calvin* Trevor," he raised his hands more in dismay than in benediction and passed silently on. I grew up to speak three languages fluently; I was also steeped in Latin and Greek; I learned sculpture at the feet of Story (I even assisted him on his great brooding Cleopatra with her asp), and painting at my father's; and I explored Rome with that brilliant friend of my youth, Marion Crawford, the future author of *Saracinesca* and so many other unforgettable romances of the old "black" papal nobility. At twenty-three I had an atelier full of my crude paintings of historical scenes à la Gérôme and an unpublished novel about Cesare Borgia. But the world was before me and I loved it.

I didn't visit my native land until the early eighteen seventies when I was sent to New York to try my hand at the untangling of the family mortgages and leaseholds, which had been mismanaged by my mother's brothers. I found that I had a head for business, despite my artistic training, and also that I was enough of a diplomat not to antagonize older relatives, and I was able to rescue enough from the general mess that I uncovered to enable my parents to continue, if more modestly, their Roman life, and for myself to sustain a just sufficiently elegant bachelor's existence in the rapidly burgeoning Fifth Avenue world of the post–Civil War boom. I liked the big, brawling brownstone city with its garish new palaces and its garish new magnates. It promised adventure, and I decided to remain, at least for a year or so. My collector's eye would make up for the deficiencies of my purse, and my social ease and demeanor could be counted on, both with the old families and the new, to attract bids for dinner parties and weekends.

I had grown up with expatriates who tended to regard Rome and Florence and Paris as the only true centers of Western art and culture, and to look down on America as intellectually a ·wasteland whose only function was to provide them with enough income to live abroad. But I could perfectly see that all this was changing and that American wealth was going to demand everything in the way of art and style and splendor of living that the old continent had to offer, and that it might be more amusing to live in a developing environment than a decaying one.

Furthermore, I enjoyed in New York what to me was the novel feeling of "belonging." I had plenty of friends in Rome, it was true, but to the Italians, at least, no matter how sympathetic and congenial, I was always at bottom a foreigner and a Protestant, as I had been Calvin to the pope. In Manhattan, where I had hosts of cousins as well as welcoming hostesses, I was "one of them," and my poise and knowledge of arts and languages made me a favorite — with the mothers and daughters, anyway. Ward McAllister, a somewhat epicene dandy who ruled the cotillions, took me up with enthusiasm and introduced me to the great, black-wigged, multi-jeweled Mrs. Astor, who affably professed herself charmed by my manners, after which there were no social peaks unassailable. I could surely now look forward to an advantageous marriage. Except, as I have said, my popularity was primarily with the mothers, rather than the fathers.

It was not that the men disliked me. Oh, they tolerated me well enough. But their world, at least their real world, into which no female could ever penetrate, was bounded on all four sides by business and law (*their* law). Even on their vacations they tended to stick together, in fishing camps and on yachting trips, where the talk was largely about money when it was not scatalogical. Newport, I discovered, was entirely run by wives and old maids; the seat at the opposite end of the hostess's at the dinner table was apt to be vacant or occupied by a distinguished foreign guest. Arts and letters had no place in the "downtown" of the goldbugs, as Henry Adams dubbed the new tycoons; such superfluities were relegated to the upper regions of urban life along with ladies' lunches and matinées and dressmakers and "uplift" lectures. And I? Well, I, of course, was that fatal thing that philistines love to call a dilettante.

I resented it deeply. Indeed, despite all my self-discipline, I have never got over resenting it. And I'm afraid my resentment has endowed me with a permanent outward defiance that has dogged me all my life, a compulsion to confirm the unfavorable opinion that many form of me, the moment I suspect them of forming it. A perfect example of this occurred at a dinner party, only some weeks past. It was a pleasant gathering of eight over a meal simply prepared and simply served, given by my physician, a widower of broad intellectual tastes, in his modest but attractively appointed brownstone. One of the guests, a renowned federal judge who had greatly enjoyed the stimulating discussion at table about the rights and wrongs of the British Empire, now fighting for its life, and who had been — at least I supposed — a bit surprised that a gentleman of my social reputation should have lent himself so easily and comfortably to the congeniality of a far from glittering evening, remarked to me as we descended the stoop afterwards: "Wasn't that a delightful party! How well everyone talked! If dining out were always like that, I guess we wouldn't hug our own hearths so tightly." To which I heard myself retort: "I have never cared for dinners served by women. If our friend can't keep a butler, he should hire one for the evening. They're not *that* expensive."

I didn't have to look around to see that the judge's features had frozen. And I had liked him, too; we had agreed so strongly that America should join the Allies! Why should I have to be so sharp with people whose only fault was that they took me for what I obviously appeared to be: a formal, immaculately clad gentleman, club man, yachtsman — whatever — from whose every pore seemed to exude the warning that he fitted into a neat cubbyhole hardly adapted to his observer's coarse and bulky figure? In the scandalous trial of Oscar Wilde some twenty years ago Lord Queensbury's successful defense to a charge of criminal libel for addressing a note to the complainant in his club — "To Oscar Wilde, posing as a sodomite" — was that the poet-playwright had at least been *posing* as one. Had I not at least been posing as what the good judge had evidently thought me?

This habit of mine hardened after my marriage. All New York had taken it quite for granted — without necessarily condemning it — that I had married for money. I had joined other eligible bachelors of the town in calling on Sunday afternoons on the five daughters of Hiram Cutter, the department store magnate, in the dark cavernous parlor of his huge brownstone cube on Fifth Avenue, whose plain facade was marred by bizarre Egyptian ornamentation. Mr. and Mrs. Cutter, however, despite the ostentation of their residence, which may have been a simple advertisement of his store, had no social ambition or need to glitter; they were stout, honest churchgoing folk who attributed their wealth to God and their general content to the regularity of their habits and the moderation of their desires. The four older daughters, all short in stature and solid in girth, were relaxed, self-confident and pleasantly plain; they obviously would — and ultimately did — make excellent wives and mothers. They were just the type to appeal to sober, industrious and ambitious young men who had no wish to appear to the eyes of the world, or to their own, as fortune hunters. And indeed every one of my four sisters-in-law made a solid and lasting match. Yet every one of them, I dare to suggest, was married basically for her money. Only my Clotilda, the youngest, was not. And, of course, it was generally believed that she was the only one who *was*. I simply looked too much the part. Why else, I could almost hear people ask, would such a dandy have wed such a dowdy?

Was she really such a dowdy? To some eyes, undoubtedly. She was tall and thin, utterly unlike her sisters, almost skinny, and her cheeks were too round, her chin too oval, her auburn hair always a bit wild, her movements awkward. But she had large beautiful light blue eyes, and her voice held conviction. And when she had occasion to move with speed, as when she jumped up and crossed the room to get something for her now ailing mother, whom she obviously adored, her action was suddenly full of grace. But perhaps the secret of her unexpected charm was the way her usual reserve gave way before any tensely sympathetic interest. She was really not shy at all, as most of the Cutter callers assumed. She had simply the good habit of taking in the world before she spoke.

As she was the youngest and least outgiving of the sisters, usually sitting in a corner bent over her needlepoint as if she preferred her solitude, I found it a simple matter to avail myself of uninterrupted colloquies with her. I not only found her rare comments much to the point; I found her silences restful and never embarrassing. Furthermore my attendance on her exempted me from the banal chatter going on in the rest of the room.

Her needlepoint, I soon discovered, had not prevented her from observing me closely. When I commented on the beauty of an Eastman Johnson conversation piece showing the Cutter family gathered before the fireplace in the parlor in which we were sitting, she observed:

"You say that with the satisfaction of a connoisseur who is glad, in a chamber of horrors, to find one object that he can honestly commend."

"You credit me, anyway, with honesty."

"Oh, yes, I think you are honest, Mr. Trevor."

"How can you be so sure?"

"By what you don't say. I watched you when Father was showing you the Bouguereau cherubs he ordered from Paris. Your face was admirably impassive, but I suspected a hidden grimace. And you never uttered a word! Not one. All the other men did. Heavens, how they lauded the wretched thing!"

"Perhaps they genuinely liked it."

"Some of them perhaps. But *all?*"

I laughed. "You mean have we really come to that? But the Johnson is not the only thing in the house that I admire. The little Corot landscape in the dining room is a gem."

"*If* it's a Corot. They're very easily faked, you know."

"Well, if it isn't a Corot, it's by a painter as good as he. But I'd stake my life on its truth. Ah, how I'd love to have painted it!"

"You do paint, don't you?"

"I daub."

"Perhaps your trouble is that your eyes are too good. You condemn everything that is not of the first rank, including your own work."

"And I shouldn't?"

"Only if you give as high marks to yourself as a critic as you give low ones to your painting."

"But what's a critic but a frustrated artist?"

"Now *that's* not worthy of you. Can Calvin Trevor be trite? The drawing rooms of Gotham will be astounded. What is a critic, a good critic, but one who takes in fully, who *receives*, a work of art? He completes the process started by the artist. He is as necessary to the artist as his paints or his brush. If Michelangelo had sculpted his *Pietà* in a forest and left it there for none to see, would it be a work of art?"

"Yes! For he would have done it for his God!"

"Then it would be a sacrifice, not an artifact."

"But you talk as if there were one critic for one artist, as if they were somehow a pair, two individuals creating a beautiful thing. Yet for every artist there may be a hundred critics, a thousand, a million! How can you claim that the million are the equal of the one?"

"Because I don't believe that the disparity is that great. I believe that a total reception of the impact of a great work of art is a very rare thing. Rare enough, anyway, for the true critic to be quite as important as the artist."

Well, needless to say, this was a point of view very gratifying to a man who prided himself on a taste not really understood by the ladies, and certainly little appreciated by the gentlemen, of contemporary Manhattan. I was intrigued by the sympathy and insight of Clotilda; I made it a point now never to miss one of the Cutter Sunday afternoons. But I was not in love with her — not yet. That happened suddenly, as such things often do, when I witnessed a brief interchange between her and her mother.

As I have said Clotilda was the baby of Mrs. Cutter's brood, and that stout amiable homely lady was not only in her sixties; she was already suffering from what was soon to be diagnosed as a fatal breast cancer. She had come over to where I was sitting with Clotilda to ask her to take a turn at serving at the tea table. Clotilda immediately jumped to her feet.

"Of course, Mama. But are you feeling tired?"

"Just a bit, my dear. Perhaps the least bit faint. I think I'll go upstairs and lie down for a minute."

"I'll go with you."

"No, dear, I'd rather you did the tea."

"Oh, Mother, please!"

At which Mrs. Cutter gratefully acquiesced, and they disappeared, the older leaning on the arm of the younger, leaving
me, as a banal poet might have put it, with my heart cleft in
twain. It was purely and simply the agony in Clotilda's "Oh,
Mother, please!" that did it, that ripped my heart. It might have
been that I had never conceived of a sympathy in another person
quite so sharp. Whatever tortures loomed for Mrs. Cutter, her
daughter would be the greater sufferer.

And I believe that was so, in the miserable year that followed.
I called almost daily at the house during Mrs. Cutter's terminal
ailment, and Clotilda would spare a half hour from her constant
vigil at the bedside to come down to the parlor to give me a
cup of tea. Our relationship had become utterly relaxed and
easy long before a word of love was exchanged between us.
When it matured into an engagement, only a few weeks after
Mrs. Cutter's demise, I was surprised only that anyone else
should have been. Of course, it was not generally known about
town how assiduous my visits to the house had been.

But surprised or not, people seemed pleased, and Mr. Cutter
was very handsome indeed about his daughter's settlements.

"We needn't bother with trusts," he told me with something
almost in the nature of a wink. "The daughters of my house
know very well how to hang on to their money."

It was inevitable that Clotilda and I should have a discussion
about this, but it did not occur until everything had been pleasantly settled.

"Your father was not like King Lear, I take it," I observed.
"He didn't make you tell him how much you loved him."

"No, he knew I would have been like Cordelia. Except
Cordelia, unlike me, knew she had a king of France in her
pocket."

"Of course, I'm no king, or anything like it, but I *would* have
taken you, like him, without a dowry."

"Dear me, what would we have lived on?"

"Well, I do have *something* of my own, you know."

"*Do* I know it? Then why, pray, are you marrying the likes of me?"

"I guess I needed more."

"And you shall have it!" She clapped her hands as if summoning a genie.

"But seriously, Clotilda, do you think me mercenary?"

"For wanting a proper *dot*? No! All good European gentlemen want that, and doesn't society here take its cue from Europe?"

"Not in that respect, anyway. Nor do I. I'd marry you tomorrow even if your father went bust."

"You'd have to, in honor. We're engaged."

"But even if we weren't."

"Heavens, how serious the man is! Very well, I'll be serious, too." Oh, the light in those clear blue eyes! But I mustn't babble. "I know, Calvin, that you love me for myself, as they say. Whatever *that* may be. God knows; *I* don't. Do any of us know what we really are?"

But I wouldn't drop it. "How can you possibly know that my love is like that?"

"Because I know that what you would really like is to marry a poor girl to show the world it was wrong about you. My riches have actually been an obstacle to you."

Her perspicacity almost appalled me. But she was going too far. I had now to be as honest as she. "But not that much of an obstacle. I'm not asking you to renounce them, am I?"

"No. Nor would I. It will be too much fun to see you enjoy them."

The truth was that she didn't really care what I felt about the money or even to what extent it might have motivated me. Once she had made up her mind that *she* loved someone, that was all she needed or wanted. I believe there were very few people in her short life whom she loved, but she made perfectly do with that small number: her mother, to a lesser extent her father, one of her sisters, a man in her past whose name I never discovered but whose existence I suspected without jealousy, myself, and, of course, more than anyone, our son, Hugh.

In the ten wonderful years of our marriage, before she was felled by the same dread disease that took away her mother, she well proved the truth of her prediction that she would enjoy watching me spend the money. She always insisted that the conversion of cash into beauty was one of the fine arts in itself, and she liked to quote the famous takeoff of Descartes's dictum: *"Je dépense, donc je suis."*

Well, I certainly had better taste than my contemporaries, but that wasn't saying much in the seventies and eighties. I had a proper horror of everything Victorian and no great passion for the French eighteenth century with which, a bit later, Ogden Codman and his ilk valiantly tried to combat it, particularly when the two were fused, as in the gilded excrescences of Newport. I was somewhat ahead of my generation in recognizing that the colonies of our prerevolutionary era had not only produced the greatest political philosophers of all time, but had raised architecture and decoration to new heights. On the banks of the Hudson near Garrison I erected a copy of Thomas Jefferson's Palladian masterpiece, Bremo, and filled it with exquisite American furniture and porcelain from the China trade. No one on our side of the Atlantic was better housed than Clotilda Trevor.

But of course the great event of our married life was Hugh. I call him an event because that was what he was from the beginning: simply the one big thing that was always happening to us. He grew up into a big tall handsome cheerful boy with thick dark curly hair and large friendly black eyes, and, after his mother's death, into the romantic image of a hero. And his character in no way belied his appearance: he was a loyal friend, in time a devoted husband and father, and, always, an incomparable son. His comprehension of me was almost uncomfortably acute; he seemed to understand my curious contrariness with strangers, and he had a way, always tactful, of stepping in to guard me, to explain me, to answer for me. There was rarely much that I could do for him in return; he seemed to educate and develop himself. At Saint Paul's School in New Hampshire he was captain of the football team and senior monitor, and at the age of seventeen he was almost in tears at being too young to enlist in the Spanish War and follow his hero, Theodore Roosevelt, in the charge up San Juan Hill. One of the last things that the dying Clotilda, sitting on a porch from which she could view the river, said to me, as she pointed to the boy below mooring his sailboat to our dock, was: "There's your immortality."

Her comment had been evoked by a discussion we had had, natural enough under the circumstances, of the survival of the soul. Clotilda was not a believer, and she faced whatever awaited her stoically, but she was troubled by my sense that nothing would survive me, neither a soul nor even the memory of any substantial accomplishment. If it troubled her, however, it did not trouble me. I was quite content to be a failure, or at least a noncontributor, in the eyes of a world whose values I did not share. Clotilda, however, insisted that I should lend some credit to *her* judgment of myself and be willing to try to see myself, Calvin Trevor, as a success in what to her was the most important of the arts: the art of living.

"For what else do we really have?" she demanded, in a tone in which I could perhaps detect a hint of desperation, for me, anyway, certainly not for herself. "What do we really have but a life? One life? If we don't make the most we can of *that*, we are really sold."

And I had the grim sense that what she meant by making the most of *her* life was making the most of mine, and that she was doubting that she had done that. Was she now trying to tell me that Hugh, at least, *would* create something, that he would do more than appreciate beautiful things and surround himself with them, and that what he created would redound in some part to the credit of his father, that in some mysterious fashion it would be an extension of something *I* had started, that he and I would be a single and durable entity?

Which brings me at last, perhaps at too long last, to the subject of Hugh and his career. What was the brilliant boy to do after his graduation from Harvard, *summa cum laude*? Many thought he should study law as a prelude to politics, which, although not considered by my friends a gentleman's occupation, had been somewhat popularized among the more idealistic young by the stirring example of Theodore Roosevelt. Others thought that his adventurous spirit would find richer territory in the field of the explorer or of the naturalist, where his ability to finance expeditions would give him a marked lead. I had a secret (for I had no wish to dominate him) hankering for archaeology, to which his passion for Greek poetry and drama might seem to point. But what he himself wanted, as he at last broke to me after the trip around the globe that followed his college graduation, was to be a poet.

I was, of course, well aware of his gift for writing clever skits for private theatricals and witty satiric poems for the birthdays and anniversaries of friends and relatives, but I had not considered this talent as the source of a career.

"I've been working in different verse forms for two years now," he informed me. "And I dare to hope at last that I'm making some progress. That month I spent in Paris on my way home, I wasn't just kicking up my heels. I was hard at work every day."

"And you've never showed me anything! Anything really serious, I mean."

"Dad, can you imagine I'd show *you* anything before I had something to show? But here it is. A sonnet series. Take it away and read it when you're by yourself and relaxed. Try to pretend they're by someone else."

"As if I could do that!"

But I was in for a blissful surprise. The sonnets, *Up the Hudson,* have, of course, been published and favorably reviewed. That a man of twenty-three should already be an accomplished poet is not in itself surprising; Keats was dead at twenty-five. But Hugh's finish, his finely chiseled work, the absence of a banal term or a flat line, even in the ever dangerous final couplet, was remarkable. The sonnets were united in theme by the poet's midsummer cruise in his sailboat up the mighty river, with glittering, shimmering passages on the verdant banks and tall hills that slipped past him. There were hints of an unhappy love affair (of which I knew nothing, as Hugh, for all the charm of his apparent candor, was a very private person), but the note most constantly stressed was of the writer's sadness that so many glorious opportunities for adventure and heroism seemed to have been exhausted by a greedy and devouring past. It was as if the poet, scanning the horizon like Tennyson's Ulysses for "some work of noble note" yet to be done, was faced only with a fat society gorging itself on the plundered fruits of a long conquered frontier. The lines inspired by the vision of West Point were particularly moving; they expressed the longing to have been at Gettysburg or in the Wilderness Campaign, the regret to have missed the chance to fight for, even to die for, the freedom of one's fellow men. The note on which the series ended was the problem of the hero into whose hand was thrust an account book rather than a sword. Might not his solution be to grasp a pen?

"You mean if I can't be Alexander I'd better content myself with being Homer?" Hugh retorted with a laugh when I offered him my interpretation. "Well, I hope I'm not quite such a muff as to imagine myself the remotest copy of either. But what I'm groping for is to find the kind of poetry that to me is innately American. These sonnets don't pretend to be that. They're simply an effort to state my problem. You see, Dad, what to me is the essence of the American saga is action. And how can I make a word an act? Sometimes I think Emerson came close to it. His sentences strike me as *things*. Do you see at all what I mean?"

"I don't, really. Wouldn't the better critics today maintain that Whitman was the quintessential American poet?"

"It's just what I claim he's not!" Hugh was moved to near indignation; he jumped up to pace the room. "All that drivel about yearning and mooning. What did he do in the war but stick bandages on wounded boys and croon over their sad fate?"

"He boasted to John Addington Symonds that he had begotten a host of bastards."

"Dad, be serious. I'm trying to tell you what sort of poetry I want to write."

"Then tell me."

"I'm trying to find out, damn it all!"

It was at this point that I began to develop my idea that Hugh might indeed have a unique offering to make to the world of art. We had been experiencing in the eighteen nineties (the Mauve Decade) and thereafter, a cultural revolution sometimes known as the "American Renaissance." Stanford White and Richard Morris Hunt were transforming New York City into a gilded reproduction of the architectural glories of Rome and Florence; Henry James was reforming the novel into a brilliant psychological study of pale American souls seen against the lurid background of Italian palazzos; Saint-Gaudens was filling our public squares with noble monuments recalling Michelangelo and Cellini; Pierpont Morgan and Isabella Gardner were rifling the treasure houses of the Old World for the benefit of our museums.

It was all very much applauded, as indeed it should have been. America had come of age, and the cultural aridity of the new continent was being blessedly irrigated by the diverted rivers of old European beauty. But that's what it was; that's my point: it was all essentially European. Oh, I'm not forgetting Irving and Hawthorne and Melville and Twain, or even Gilbert Stuart or the Peales or Copley (though he emigrated), but they all looked a bit provincial, a bit primitive, in the splendor of the new imports. Did the great Yankee dames of the era go to Eakins or Eastman Johnson for their portraits? No, they went to that able son of confirmed expatriates, John Singer Sargent, or even to the insidiously clever Boldini.

My only real gripe with all this — foreign born and bred as I was — was that the one type of man whom both the Europe lovers and the down-to-earth Americans united to deplore was the one who understood just what art was all about, on both sides of the Atlantic, and just what was worth emulating or collecting, the man who, without being himself a creator, knew how to separate the chaff from the wheat among objects aspiring to be beautiful. But did they call him what he was, a critic? Oh, no, they called him a dilettante!

You will see him in a hundred caricatures of the period, willowy, falsely elegant and suave, raising his monocle disdainfully before downgrading something of whose loveliness he is less unaware than jealous. You will see him as a near villain in the fiction of James and Edith Wharton and as an actual one in melodramas. And yet who else was it who stood between all the true artists and the basic indifference or even scorn of the public? For how much did the masses care that anyone wanted or needed art? How much did God?

Of course, any reader will sense the strong, the even perhaps monotonously repeated note of personal resentment in the last paragraph. Obviously I am well aware that I have been condemned as just such a dilettante by even my close friends in artistic and literary circles in New York and, no doubt, endowed with all the qualities of shallowness and heartlessness that curiously seem to accompany, in the eyes of one's observers, any recognition of innate good taste. Is it possibly because the artist — and I speak now of the artist of the American Renaissance — may feel, perhaps unconsciously, that there is something meretricious in his rapacious borrowing from old Europe, which can be redeemed only by purging, in his recreations, the evil of the past? Thus Hunt may have felt that he had redeemed a Genovese palace, the seat of unknown cruelties and horrors, by converting it into an innocent Newport summer villa. But those who have *not* been a part of the act of purgation, those, like myself, who, without having partaken of the bread and wine of redemptive recreation, dine in the villa and are aware only of the vastly superior beauty of its model in Italy, are still imbued with the wickedness of the latter and damned as dilettantes!

Fired, at any rate, with my new conception of what Hugh might attain, seeing him, in short, as nothing less than the long-needed bridge between two cultures, as the poet who might create a new and essentially American art form where the European word, so to speak, and the American act would be as one, I backed his project with my heartiest approval. He didn't, of course, have any need of my financial support, though every penny I had was always at his free disposal, but he had always manifested a strong need for my support in any project that he entertained. He told me, as I have said, that he had not dared to show me a line of his serious poetry until he felt that he had some mastery of his craft. He may have been endowed, perhaps by his mother, with an unreasonably high regard for the powers of my critical faculties.

If he cared for my opinion of his art, however, it was just the opposite with his girlfriends. He always wanted me to like them, it is true, and he made sure that I had ample occasion to meet and appraise them, but it was very clear that in this field he must choose for himself. I liked, at least at first, the one he married, Vivian Bell, but I think I always knew that she and I were not doomed to love each other. As I have already suggested, she was very much the independent, high-spirited, innovative, privileged (and serenely content to be so) "Gibson" girl of the period: beautiful, willful, impatient with anything or anyone standing in her way, including a father-in-law. I could see that in many ways she was the ideal mate for Hugh, but I did not like the obvious fact that she fully intended to have at least an equal share with him in the making of every important decision in his life. And his choice of career was certainly the first of these.

This was put off, anyway, for the full year of their honeymoon, which took them to the South Sea Islands, Australia and India. On their return they were invited to spend a weekend at the White House by the "Princess Alice," President Roosevelt's daughter by his first marriage, soon to be wed to Nicholas Longworth and a stout friend of Vivian, whose spirit was as lively as her own. Hugh, of course, was a passionate admirer of the hero of San Juan Hill, and the great man, little to my surprise, took an immediate interest in my son, holding him up to his own boys as a fine example of a Harvard graduate. And it was only to be expected that he wouldn't hear of Hugh's adopting any career but a political one.

"Poetry is bully," he conceded, "but it need hardly take up all of a man's time. Nobody can fault me in my esteem for the world of letters. Reading with me is a *disease*. And look how many books I've written! But a man, my dear Hugh, cannot afford just to sit and scribble while the stink of the Augean stables assails his nostrils. He must pick up a shovel and tackle the eternal job of cleaning them out!"

Coming from whom it came, this advice had some effect on Hugh, determined though he was to carry out his original purpose. Vivian, however, in strongly backing the president, overplayed her hand, causing a reaction of some stubbornness in her husband. When Hugh discussed the question with me, he had made sure we were alone.

"Roosevelt's faith in himself is unbounded," I pointed out. "And of course such a man can always create the illusion that a great executive can really accomplish something. But can he? Can any president? Isn't he like a man making a clearing in the jungle? If he wades into the dense swamp of red tape and shouts enough orders and waves his arms about, he may at last effect some kind of open space. But when the shouting and the shaking die, the thick green bureaucracy will ineluctably reclaim its own."

"So nothing's really worth it in politics, is that it, Dad?"

"Well, you may recall Anatole France's tale of how Louis-Napoléon, armed with all the trappings of absolute dictatorship, was still unable to obtain a petty governmental office for the son of his old wet nurse."

"You think, in short, that I should stick to my rhymes?"

"I most certainly do. And I'd be willing to make a large wager that Anatole France will be remembered long after Napoléon III is forgotten."

"You really think I have it in me, Dad? Really and truly? Cross your heart and hope to die, as you used to say to me when I was a boy?"

What a searing pain it gives me now to remember those

burning black eyes in that beautiful pale countenance! How could any man who looked so much like a poet, like a romantic Victorian drawing of the dead Byron, really be one? Was I acting in a *play* about a poet? What madness was it in me that drove me to try to *be* my son, simply to partake of the atmosphere he breathed?

Silently, to answer him, I drew my forefinger in two lines across my chest.

He took a couple of steps away from me, his eyes on the floor. "Keats hoped that he might be included among the British poets. If I could have the tiniest spot among the Americans!"

The rest of his story, though it covered some half dozen years, is soon told. I make it brief because my own role in it was minimal. Vivian's influence was now paramount. I do not say that it was she who encouraged him to go on the fatal expedition in Brazil with the ex-president in 1913, but it was certainly she who applauded his giving up poetry for exploration.

Not that she was wholly wrong about the poetry. I have reached an age where, if you can't at least try to be fair, what are you? Hugh and Vivian engaged Frank Lloyd Wright to build them a dramatic rock cottage on a cliff overlooking the Hudson, and they divided their year between this and a ranch in Cuba. It was in the latter place that he composed most of his long epic, *Remember the Maine.*

He wouldn't let me read a single couplet until it was finished. There were certainly a great many of these, heroic ones, too, each one an enclosed, a perfect, entity. I recalled his admiration of Emerson and what he had described as the great essayist's ability to make every sentence a "thing." Hugh's was indeed a remarkable accomplishment, but the cumulative effect was . . . lapidary. There. I've said it.

The subject, if bleak, was at least poetically promising.

Everything that was sordid about the Spanish War, from the Hearst-inspired jingoism of the American press to the brutal imperialism of Madrid, was grimly set forth; no good could come of it, and no good, according to the poet, ever did. Yet the spirit and courage of the Rough Riders made the statement that there were still values in men that rendered the species not totally useless.

It was a dark conclusion to a dark epic. I wonder if Hugh would have derived much comfort today from the spirit of men dying by the thousands — nay, by the hundreds of thousands — in the trenches in France. But what good is going to come out of *that?* At any rate, his poem was faultless. Except in the all-encompassing fault of being dull.

Nobody recognized this sooner than Hugh himself. His good sportsmanship was as evident as on the rare occasions when he lost a tennis match. He leaped almost cheerfully over the net of literature to grasp the hands of the critics who had damned him. And he and Vivian, leaving the two children in the good care of her parents, took off on a six-month trip to study the giant lizards of Komodo.

The expedition led to further ones, on which Vivian, as a dutiful mother, could not accompany him. There was an attempt to scale Mount Everest, which failed; there was a scientific excursion to Antarctica, and finally there was the fatal trip to explore the River of Doubt, a tributary of the Amazon, with the ex-president and his son Kermit.

We shall never know if Hugh's two heart attacks, the second of which was fatal, and which occurred only a few months after his return from Brazil, were triggered by the malaria that he contracted in the jungle, or by some strange insect bite, but Hugh had seemed in perfect health before the ill-fated trip on which two of the expeditionary force had died and the great Theodore himself had almost lost his life. At one point indeed the ailing and aging Rough Rider, who now had to be carried, had urged his companions to leave him to die and press on to save themselves. Needless to say this heroic and utterly sincere plea had fallen on deaf ears.

There can be no more fitting epitaph than what Hugh told me about this last episode in the hospital after his first attack and just before the final second.

"I must tell you, Dad, that I sympathized with the president's wish. I was convinced that he was really about to die, and I didn't see why he shouldn't be allowed to do so in peace. But I had no idea of leaving him; I would remain and die with him. If the others dragged me on, I would escape from them at night and return to the old hero. Of course, I can see now that my own fever was so high that I was getting everything all wrong and that otherwise I would never have dreamed of the possibility of those men leaving the president. And we all did get out, of course. But what a glorious end it would have been! Dying at the side of the great man who had believed there was nothing he could not accomplish! And yet who was coming at last to a defiant end in a remorselessly indifferent jungle, surrounded by animals and plants that had no function but to devour each other! What a poem! What an epic! Wasn't that the *Hyperion* that Keats left unfinished? Where life at last became art!"

My dear wife had wanted me to feel the ultimate success of my life in Hugh's. Is it tragic, or simply pathetic, that I should feel my ultimate failure in his?

The Last of the
Great Courtesans

RECEIVING THE COMMISSION for Millamant (Milly) Marion's portrait was a signal honor for me, as Marion Enterprises, the media giant, could command the highest-priced painter in Manhattan for a likeness of its beautiful chairwoman to adorn its boardroom. Milly, of course, was not quite the beauty she had been; she was exactly my age, having been born in 1917, and was now, though her admirers could hardly believe it, a good sixty years of age. There had been those of us who had thought, when she was young, that her almost movie-star blond prettiness might not bear the years well, but they had been proven ludicrously wrong. Milly's curly gold hair, however supplemented by art, her gray-blue eyes that seemed laughingly to mock you, her small delicately carved features and the pursed lips from which could emerge so surprisingly raucous a laugh, all topping a long, thin, lissome, easily striding figure, made her even more remarkable than she had been in the full flower of youth.

At Yale, at least in Pierpont College, we had all been in love with her. Her father, Endicott Iglehart, master of the college and beloved professor of English, had named her after Millamant, his favorite heroine in Congreve's *The Way of the World,* inevitably by all but him shortened to Milly, and from her earliest days she had demonstrated the bewitching charm of her namesake. Iglehart was famous for his dramatic lectures on the English romantic poets; his big crowded classroom would be reverently silent when his rich mellow tones almost broke in recounting the last days of the consumptive Keats in his rooms over the Spanish Steps or the drowning of Shelley in the Bay of Spezzia. A cynic even in youth, I was inclined to snicker to myself at the old boy's act, and I wasn't the only one to note that the adulatory group of undergraduates who were invited to the choicer gatherings at the master's house was made up not only of class leaders, such as the elect of the secret society, Skull & Bones, but of the socially élite, such as those who had been tapped for the less prestigious but tonier Scroll & Key, scions of gold coasts. Oh, yes, Professor Iglehart, for all of his perfectly genuine love of letters — and a fine life of Wordsworth stands to his credit — was a snob, but then who is without some touch of that minor vice, in one field or other? The renowned Jowett of Balliol College in Oxford was one of the greatest of Greek scholars, yet it was known that he dearly loved a peer. Jowett had no children of his own to be affected by his attitude, but Iglehart had Milly.

My wife, Georgia, was not altogether pleased when I told her that Milly was coming to my studio to sit for me. She was too sensible to have any real apprehension that the "puppy love," as she dubbed it, which I had felt for the master's daughter in my junior year in New Haven was going to flare up four decades later, but Milly's enduring beauty and reputation with men were not matters that a loving wife could totally discount.

"Maybe I should bring a book or a crossword and sit in on your sessions," she suggested, with a touch of dryness.

"Milly would be *so* flattered."

"Exactly. That's why I shan't do it. But tell me, Larry. What do you really think of her? What is under all that charm and poise? Has she a heart at all? How do you judge her?"

I shrugged. "I guess I don't. I'm like that pope in Rome who, when told of Cardinal Richelieu's death, remarked: 'Well, if there's a God, he'll have much to answer for. If not . . . well, he led a successful life.' "

"That's all very well for a pope. A pope of *those* days. What a difference! I might have even been a Catholic then. But sticking to this life, has hers really been successful? Or is it all an act?"

"If it is, it's a pretty good one. Everyone admires her."

"Not this chicken!"

"I should have said every man."

"And what do they know about her? If she runs for Congress, as they say she might, she may have reason to regret the Nineteenth Amendment."

Milly, arriving in my studio the day after this little chat, treated me to an act that I was presumably meant to interpret as that of the charming little girl, entranced at being admitted to the sanctum sanctorum of the great artist whom, however, she knows too well not to spoof. She went at once to the stack of canvases against the wall and, without asking leave, began turning them over to examine them.

"Good heavens, is that Sybil Dale? Why are you doing that old cow? And what on earth have you done with her second chin? And is this really Steve Kennedy? Did he leave his pot in the lobby? And really, Larry, who in God's name is this pompous little man in the white coat who looks as if he's looking for something?"

"He's probably looking for a cavity. He's a famous dentist. At least I think that's he." I approached for a better look. She was between me and the canvases.

"You don't even *know*! You're doing too many of them! If you don't watch out, you'll be getting slick. Maybe I've come to you too late! I can hear you, if the next sitter asks who I am: 'Oh, some cocktail waitress.' "

"Cocktail waitresses can't afford me."

"Not while they're still cocktail waitresses!"

"Milly, will you please sit down. We must find the right pose."

I chose at last one in which she was seated, leaning slightly forward in a Louis XV bergère, her face tilted back as she smiled up at what the viewer might imagine to be a standing and admiring male. She was relieved when I told her that I had no objection to chatting sitters.

"It's better than having them impatiently silent. To me it's a kind of background music."

"You mean you don't have to listen."

"Well, I do, more or less. Except in moments of greatest concentration."

"It's like psychoanalysis, then. I remember my own. I don't believe Doctor Slesnik heard more than half of what I said. I think he was doing a crossword. But a painter at least has to be looking at you. And so intently! And imagine having one like you who has known me so long and so well! It's really rather chilling. What can I hide?"

"You've never struck me, Milly, as one who's taken much trouble to hide things."

"Ah, so you think me bold, brash?"

"Isn't 'honest' the term?"

"Why, thank you, Larry! A compliment from you really means something. I feel you see me through and through."

"I didn't always."

"When did you not?"

I suddenly saw an expression that I wanted in the way she raised her eyebrows, and I made a few quick strokes on the canvas. The act may have jostled out a thought I had not wished to express. "When I was in love with you. Back in the Yale days. Of course, then I saw you in a golden haze."

"Oh, come now, you were never very far gone, my dear. You recovered pretty fast."

"I had no alternative. You had eyes only for Paul Kelly."

"Could you blame me?"

"Because he was tall and handsome and captain of the football team? No, I guess he was irresistible. But I had idealized you. I had hoped you wanted more than that. A crusader, a pioneer, a poet."

"Why not a painter?"

"Well, that was only my dream then."

"Don't tell me that. You were always at it. Remember? Incomprehensible abstracts, too, in those days. I thought you'd spend your life in a garret, happily daubing away. It didn't help you with me, either. What girl wants that for a life?"

"You wanted the great world? Even back then?"

There was a flash of impatience in her eyes at this. "None of you understood what it was like to be Daddy's daughter at Yale. It's all very well to say it should have been a happy position, with him so loved and popular and surrounded by the élite of the students, and myself possessed of decent looks and a party manner. But those things aren't everything."

"I should have thought they almost were." I had found my start for the picture and was content to work in silence now that I had given her a theme for a monologue.

"Well, *you* were the first to hint to me that Daddy was a terrible old snob. Oh, you thought you did it so subtly, but at the age we were then, we used only meat axes. And of course, you were totally right. And of course I knew it. Daddy's criterion in selecting his disciples was far from simply literary. He, and Mother, too, for all her plain, down-to-earth quality, placed a great if unspoken emphasis on style, on looks, on urbanity, on social ease. And yes, even on athletics. I remember how Daddy would complain, during the war, when the senior class was decimated by it and he had largely 4-F men to teach, that he had learned the truth of the old adage of a sound mind in a sound body! And I don't have to tell you, who observed everything, how many of his golden youths came from golden backgrounds. When I was invited to weekends by my beaux in Southampton or Tuxedo or Westbury I could hardly be unaware of the difference between their estates and our shabby gentility in New Haven. Oh, the Igleharts may have been what is called old stock, sure, but Daddy's salary made up most of our income, and you know what they paid professors in those days. And I had five kid brothers and sisters! Oh, I can tell you, when I got a new ball gown, it was an event. I had to wear it again and again!"

"But you always dazzled."

"Well, I had to do *something* so people wouldn't notice my repeats. Though of course men never do. And I learned early how to cope with my own sex. Show them frankly that you know you're not getting away with anything, and they'll forgive. But it's true that by the time you came on the scene I had already pretty well made up my mind that Paul was the man for me. Even though I found Larry Hyde quite cute."

"Thanks for the consolation prize."

"Well, Paul did seem to have everything. And in sober fact he did. He was much more than a jock. He loved poetry and history. He graduated *cum laude*. He had background, and even money, or at least the right start to make it. And character, too."

"And your parents obviously approved."

"Only too much so! It was embarrassing. Father was in heaven. Or at least on the brink. He could have chanted his Nunc Dimittis."

"Tell me something, Milly." I lowered my brush for a moment. "Why wasn't Paul everything that *you* wanted, too? Even after you married him?"

"He was everything that I had *thought* I wanted. And one of the many ironies in my life is that he has ended up as rich as even I could wish. Of course, at the time of our divorce one couldn't have predicted that he would do quite as well as he has in Morgan Stanley, but one knew he was doing okay. No, that wasn't it."

"It was you, then, who changed."

"It was I. Oh, I plead guilty. You needn't look at me in that prosecutorial way. Life with Paul showed me how limited my ambition had been. It was precisely what I had visualized. We had a fine child, only one, which, by the way, was my fault, a daughter, and Paul was enough of a gent to claim he had always wanted a daughter, and she adored him, and still does. We had a charming little house in Westbury and agreeable friends and an active social life. On the weekends we played golf and tennis and bridge, and I did the usual stint of fundraising for charities and hospital visiting. There was really nothing much to rebel against. Our friends, lawyers and bankers and brokers and their wives, usually with parents much richer than themselves, all of established families, were conservative but not meanly so. They had some civic conscience and disapproved of people who were too crudely racist. They were 'nice.' That is the word I keep coming back to. God, we were nice!"

"You were bored."

"No, it wasn't that. Those people weren't really dull. Paul wasn't dull. What I felt . . . how can I put it? As if I'd learned all the rules of a game that I now found I didn't really want to play. It wasn't such a bad game — it was quite a good one, in fact, as games go — but it wasn't *my* game. And then, before I had even started to make up my mind what I was going to do about it, the war came, and Paul, who had a reserve commission, went off into the Atlantic on a destroyer. The war not only disrupted my life. In a way it put an end to it."

"It did that literally for millions."

"It also brought new life. Of different kinds. To some it brought guts and courage they never dreamt they had. To others it uncovered the beast in them."

"And which happened to you?"

"Ah, the prosecutor again! How you frown! Well, for two years nothing much happened to me. I moved into town, got a job in Red Cross and spent a couple of evenings a week acting as a hostess in an officers' service club. Paul came home once on a month's leave. Time passed. And then in 1944 I met Eric Moore."

My eyes were now focused on the canvas. I did not trust myself to comment.

"Oh, how I see you condemn me, Larry! To have cheated on a husband overseas! How low can a bitch fall?"

"Well, I was a husband overseas myself. I can imagine what Paul must have gone through when he found out."

"Does it help my case any that Paul at the time was safe as a church as commander of a channel port base in England and that Eric was killed as a paratrooper when he dropped into Normandie?"

"Not at all! Paul was transferred against his will from his destroyer when the base needed an immediate new command. And the other man's death, like millions of others in the war, has nothing to do with the price of eggs!"

"I guess I'll have to grant you that. But let me go on."

"*You* were the one who interrupted yourself."

"I know. It shows I'm desperate, doesn't it? I'm trying to get some of that frown off your face. You never knew Eric. He was in many ways Paul's opposite. Short, almost ugly, but strong, rough. His father had been a policeman, and he had made his way up in the world as an engineer. He was amazingly competent; he could do anything. He had already been dropped twice into France to join the Resistance, and he was over here to train paratroopers at Fort Ordway in Jersey for the great invasion. When he took me out there one day and his jeep broke down and the driver couldn't fix it, he jumped out, slipped under the car and repaired in a minute whatever had to be repaired. And when he got up out of the dusty road there wasn't a spot on him! Does that give you a picture?"

"Uh-huh. Where did you meet him?"

"At the officers' club. He propositioned me the first night. I brushed him off, but I found him in the lobby of my apartment house the next day. He had a few days' leave, and he attached himself to me like a bulldog. His attraction was strong, and I'm afraid I didn't hold out very long. He was completely amoral — at least so far as sex was concerned. He believed that our reproductive instincts were given us to be gratified regardless of prior commitments. He had no qualms about Paul; he even said: 'If he's living chastely in Falmouth, he's a fool.' Nor did he ever so much as whisper a word about love."

"But no doubt his deeds made up for his words."

"He was certainly a highly competent lover. And I don't mind telling you that he taught me a few things that a gal finds handy to know when she's faced with the job of holding the interest of an elderly and fickle tycoon."

So we *were* going to get around to Randolph Marion. I had suspected as much. "A job, you call it?"

"Well, women like me — if there really *are* any women quite like me — have to add brains to their other charms. You remember Madame de Pompadour and Louis XV: she was always at her wit's end to keep him amused. Some historians say she was sexually cold. I can well believe it. It takes a certain coolness to hold a naturally lascivious man for twenty years."

"But not exclusively. She ran a brothel for him."

"Brothel?" Milly wrinkled her nose. "The *Parc aux Cerfs*? It was a very choice, very tidy affair. And for the king only. That was where Madame's brains came in."

"And when she died, probably of exhaustion from entertaining him, the old boar sated himself with that hot little tramp, DuBarry. I guess nobody called *her* cool!"

"But the king was old then. Any piece of meat would do."

"As long as we're going into this, Milly, do you mind if I ask you a very personal question?"

"Of course not."

"Wasn't Paul a perfectly competent lover?"

"He was. Very male. But with Eric I was in the hands of a master. For all his toughness and crudeness, he had an extraordinary sensitivity as to what a woman wants. It was as if he might have had, however well concealed, some female chromosomes in his make-up. Perhaps the perfect male lover must have a few. Poor Paul didn't have any."

" 'Poor Paul'? Were you in love with Eric?"

"I don't really know. I was utterly subjugated by him during our brief affair. I made no effort to conceal it, and of course Paul was told. But when I learned of Eric's death, curiously enough, I wasn't crushed. It was as if I had known it was all over between us when he went away. The only tribute I paid him was in my refusal to make up with Paul when he came home after V-J Day. He had learned of Eric's fate and had decided to take a noble stand of forgiveness. But I would have none of it. I wanted a divorce and a new life."

"Why?"

"I wanted to see what would happen to this new Milly. At any price! And I paid the price, too! I asked for no alimony and received none. I let Paul divorce me for adultery here in New York and didn't even oppose his getting custody of Stella. I turned a deaf ear to the shrill cries of my parents and siblings, who called me a scarlet woman and a disgrace to the family! I think I even welcomed it all! I felt something like the wild ecstasy of Salome when she kisses the lips of the severed head of the Baptist! I was alive, Larry! Can you see that?"

"But what did you live on in those days?"

"I had men friends. Even some important ones. I 'borrowed' from them. But most of all, I went to work. I became, in rapid succession, the assistant society editor of *Style Magazine*, then the society editor, then the fashion editor and at last the editor. My particular helper, Murray Bell, whose position I took on his retirement, was also my particular triumph, as his normal taste was for the boys. But snobbishness is the strongest power on earth, mightier than sex, and he had to have the woman who had become the symbol of female allure in his tight little world. He saw to it that my new penthouse was decorated by the greatest decorators, and all for nothing, and that my parties were the smartest in Manhattan. And all the while I had my eye on one man."

"Randolph Marion."

"There you are. He owned the whole media empire of which *Style* was only a cog. But he took an interest in that cog as a testing ground of the tastes of the American female on whose approval so much of his empire depended, and he treated me as a kind of interpreter of my sex long before we became intimate.

To me he was simply the ideal man, the man I had been looking for to make sense of a world that had made none to me. He was large, and handsome for his age, which was sixty when we met. But of course you know how he looked. Everyone does. He regarded the world before him squarely and dispassionately, to see just where and how it could be had. Power was his single obsession; its quest and seizure the only activities that provided anything like a permanent satisfaction for him. And there was always more power to be had. The game — and a thrilling game it was — never ended. What he felt for his wife, his children, his friends and business associates, and, yes, even me, was a cool, superior, mildly amused amiability. We were not worth losing his temper over. As a matter of fact, I never saw him lose his temper. If something went wrong, if, say, a proposed takeover of a periodical or radio station fell through, he simply turned away from it and never mentioned it again."

"And for his victims? What did he feel for them?"

"You mean the officers of companies he bought? He often reemployed them. But if they were too bitter, he simply forgot about them. After all, he had beat them fairly — at least by his lights, for it was one of the rules of his game never to violate the letter of the law."

"Only the letter?"

"Well, he used to say that laws didn't contain anything *but* the letter. That they couldn't have any spirit as they were passed by legislatures that often hadn't even read them. They existed only to be got around, and getting around them was the business of lawyers, of whom he hired the best."

"Had he no ideals? No ambition to create a great magazine or a great paper? What was it all for?"

"To give the public what it wanted! He said they always ended by getting it, anyway. The only trick was to be the one who supplied it. But that trick was the game that made life worth living. Insofar as it was."

"And how did you fit into his game?"

"I amused him. And I learned how to *keep* amusing him. It helped me, too, that he was getting older, and one of the characteristics of his way of getting older was that he disliked any changes in the people around him. This, however, worked to my disadvantage in one respect. He refused even to discuss divorcing the wife from whom he had long been separated. He liked things just as they were, acting, when he chose to visit me, as a kind of silently critical host at the parties I gave in the town house he bought for me or the great country place he leased in Manhasset. I had a position similar to what was known in the court at Versailles as the *maîtresse en titre*."

"And what finally changed that?"

"His first stroke. He had never anticipated that anything like that could happen to him. He had always expected to be in perfect control of his businesses and people. And now he was in a wheelchair. Oh, his mind was still there, or most of it, anyway, but he couldn't bear to have people see him, and he needed an agent to stand between him and the world and convey his wishes and commands to it. It was here that he found me indispensable. I understood a lot about his work and all about his pleasures; I knew his business associates and his children; I could run his house and be with him twenty-four hours a day. But I had a condition. He had to marry me."

"Why, in view of what you and he had been to each other, was that so important?"

"Because he owed it to me! It was time that he gave me a full acknowledgement of my role in his life. Oh, he resisted it! But when he saw that I really meant it, that I would walk out if he didn't give me what I asked, he gave in. And once he did that, he did it handsomely. He not only married me; he changed his will to make me his sole residuary legatee."

"A lot of people thought that was a bit excessive."

"Oh, the family tried to break the will when he died. As everyone who reads the tabloids knows. But I bought them off cheaply enough. They already had millions from him, Larry! Millions! Randolph knew exactly what he was doing. He hated taxes, and the marital deduction meant his estate wouldn't have to pay any. *I* was the only way his empire could be kept intact. And it has been!"

I turned from the canvas to gaze at her, almost in awe. I quoted Banquo. " 'Thou hast it now: King, Cawdor, Glamis, all.' "

Her reply came sharply back; she was not for nothing Professor Iglehart's daughter. "But you fear I played 'most foully' for it? How? I never told Randolph an untruth. I don't think I ever hid a thing from him. We were entirely frank with each other. I even promised him that I would leave a good portion of my estate back to his family. *Unless* I chose to give it all away in my lifetime. To charity, of course. He agreed to it. None of that, of course, was in writing. He trusted me and my discretion. And he was right to do so."

"What about your daughter? Won't you settle a fortune on her?"

"On Stella? Heavens, no. She told me roundly that she'd never take a penny of Marion's money. She said it was whore's pay."

"Milly! She couldn't have!"

"Oh, but she did. And not angrily, either, but in a cold, clinical tone. She professes to regard me as an interesting case history. As the last, as she almost flatteringly puts it, of the great courtesans. The last of the women who were forced to use their sexual allure, or what they managed to make seem that, as the only tool available to wrest from males some fraction of the worldly loot they had grabbed for themselves. So I am to join the lovely (I hope) ladies of Villon's song, Flora and Thaïs, with the snows of yesteryear. It's nice, I suppose, to have been the last of something. The first have to fight too hard."

"As Stella may be finding out."

"You mean in getting one of those dreary jobs that men used to deny her? As an accountant or taxidermist or dentist or what have you? She won't have to fight so hard. Plenty of men must be glad to give them up. Or should be. Anyway, I'm glad I lived when I did. Maybe women like me are on the way out, but, God, are we going to be missed!"

"Is that what I'm to put in your portrait?"

"Why not? It's a great idea!"

I gave it due reflection in the sittings that followed. I reviewed in my mind some of the great portraits of famous mistresses of the past: Romney's Lady Hamilton, Boucher's Madame de Pompadour, the anonymous nude likeness of Diane de Poitiers. But the image that came most to mind was one of a woman who hadn't been a mistress at all, but a wife, and, so far as we know, an eminently respectable one, Sargent's portrait of Mrs. Hugh Hammersly, consort of a rich London stockbroker, seated in glorious red against a gilded background, beautiful, with a charming smile, warmly greeting an unseen visitor — yet somehow inconsequential. Because she was so married? Henry Adams, seeing the portrait at the great Chicago Exposition, opined that Sargent was showing the shallow soul of the wife of the "goldbug." His picture was the portrait of an era, and one that neither Adams nor Sargent admired. Was that what happened to the courtesan when she became a wife, as indeed had Milly? When becoming a wife, after all, had been the thing she had been really after? So that she could rank, with her plunder, among the mightiest of males?

My portrait of the beautiful Milly has been considered by some critics as my major achievement. Only two or three have noted that the motif of gleaming gold, sounded in a curl of her hair, picked up in an earring, repeated in the buckle of her belt and ablaze in her evening slippers, almost audibly chinks.

The Devil and Guy Lansing

I ADDRESS YOU as "Most Excellent Theophilus," meaning Beloved of God, my dear Robert, as that is the salutation of Saint Luke, namesake of our cherished school, in the third verse of his Gospel. It is not, I hasten to assure you, that I am posing as an evangelist. Far from it, as far as can be. This communication will be neither a gospel nor an apostolic epistle, but it will deal with heresy, or at least the illusion of heresy, which may lend it a quasi-ecclesiastical tint. I am still an Episcopal priest, even if I became so only to qualify for the headmastership towards which glittering goal you were sufficiently inspired, or sufficiently deluded, to direct my admittedly eager steps.

There! That is my first confession. There will be others. And into your hands I confer the decision as to whether I should resign the high post that you and your then compliant board of trustees conferred upon me five years ago, in the same fatal year that witnessed the first resignation of an American president. The second decision, whether I should at the same time submit my demission as a cleric, will be my own, but it most likely will be consistent with yours. It seems to me that having so long regarded the two roles as essentially one, they should stand or fall together.

You may think I am expecting a lot of you. You may well ask

{ 98 }

why, when you have stood so staunchly behind the unhappy Guy Lansing to defeat last year's attempted coup to oust me by that fierce little group of suddenly dissentient board members, you should now be called upon to resift the evidence and reconsider your judgment. It is simply because my conscience, my bullying, importunate, even impertinent, perhaps conscienceless conscience, keeps prodding me to make sure that *all* the facts — or even all the fantasies — are before you.

You are, I believe, some fifteen years my senior, having been born, if memory serves, in 1918. As a boy at Saint Luke's you saw it still essentially under the same regime as had existed at its founding in the last century: a private New England church school, all boys, all boarders, with only a handful of Catholics and no Jewish or black students, drawn largely from established and affluent families of Boston, New York and Philadelphia. The emphasis was heavily on God and competitive sports, though the academic side was not slighted, particularly where Latin and Greek were concerned. The aim was to train the sons of privilege to be leaders. It was to some extent a copy of the English public school, without the hierarchical snobbery or the buggery. As you once put it: "No peers or pederasts."

Your clear eye distinguished what was good in the olio from what was bad. Or to change the metaphor, you were never one to jettison the baby with the bathwater. You did not sneer at the school, as some "liberal" graduates have done, wrapping themselves smugly in the sexual license and agnosticism of a new day. You perceived that Saint Luke's could be stripped of the cloying garments of a dated Victorianism and reclothed in the best — if best there were — of our time. And you selected me to be your agent of change.

Which is why I want you to see Guy Lansing as vividly as I am beginning to see myself.

To do this I must briefly review my life, at least up to the time when as a young master, as well as a graduate of the school, I first came to your attention as a possible head. Forgive me if some of the facts are already known to you from what I suppose must have been a fairly comprehensive background check before my appointment. One never knows what may have been left out.

My father died of cancer when he was only forty and I ten, his career as a brilliant and liberal Episcopal preacher at Trinity Church in Boston cut short at the very time when he was, in the opinion of his most esteemed contemporaries, on the verge of stepping into national renown. My poor mother was left a shattered relict with small means and an only child in whom she placed all her hopes for a restoration of the golden world that had so dismally failed her.

I think of Mother as she was when she died, at only fifty, like my father of cancer: thin and bony yet somehow noble, with rather haggard eyes and long, never well groomed hair, trying unsuccessfully to disguise from an adored son her many concerns about the present and future. The curious thing about her, it strikes me as I look back, is that, high-minded and rigidly ethical herself, she never seemed to find it necessary to inculcate moral principles in me, even though it was obvious that her goal for me was worldly success. By this I do not mean just riches or power. Mother would have settled for any success, literary, academic, financial or mercantile, that would have given me a famous but honorable name. And she must have counted on me for the honorable. At the risk of sacrilege I would dare to suggest that she was like the Virgin who knew she need have no concern over the Christ child's morals.

I was sent to Saint Luke's thanks to the generosity of an old cousin of my father's who was a devoted graduate. Mother was not only adept but shameless at seeking out such resources among the multitudinous family connections. Anyway, it was worth it. My five years at the school were perhaps the happiest and sunniest of my life. It may be harsh to say it, but home with my bereaved parent and her grim older maiden sister was not a cheerful place. At Saint Luke's I came into my own. If unhappy school days are a prerequisite to the flowering of genius, if a Dotheboys Hall is necessary to the burgeoning of talent, then I have missed my opportunity. The beauty of the school, a Palladian symphony of red brick and white columns and emerald lawns, dominated by the great tower of its fine gray Gothic chapel, entered into my soul.

And I was popular. I was an able rower; I attained high grades; I became an editor of the school paper and a prefect of my class. Many of the boys came from wealthy homes providing diversions that they sometimes fretfully missed in the monastic atmosphere of a church school in a cold Massachusetts winter, but to me Saint Luke's was all that it purported to be: the happy training ground of idealistic youths who wanted to grow up into men who would make a better world.

Oh, yes, there *were* boys like me then. I sometimes wonder how much good they have accomplished. But I anticipate my theme.

And now I come to Mr. Mount. Stuyvesant Mount, or "Mounty" as the boys called him behind his back. He played so strong a role in the recent plot to get rid of me that I may as well deal with him at this point. Of course, he was already a master when I came to the school at the age of thirteen, head of the classics department and in his late or middle thirties. But he looked very much as he still looks today: short, round and stout with short, gray (then premature) hair parted neatly in the middle, a circular bland countenance that could be either beamingly Pickwickian in benevolence or Jovian in one of his terrible temper tantrums, a waddling gait and a waggish sense of humor until a sudden reminder of his own dignity and God's awful presence struck him. He had already made himself something of a school institution; he had published his own edition of Caesar's *Commentaries* and was revered as an inspiring teacher who could make at least the brighter boys aware that there was beauty in the odes of Horace. And he was popular, too, in his own special way, except for those unfortunates who had encountered his rare but thunderous wrath. The mere menace of this was enough to enable him to maintain a strict discipline even with those students most inclined to be rowdy. Mounty was never a master to fool with.

He had favorites, and I was one of them. Almost all of these (except for an occasional star Latin student) were handsome and athletic boys, and he was prone to patting one's shoulder, adjusting one's tie or collar, brushing something off one's jacket, any small gesture to justify physical proximity. I was a handsome enough fellow — there's no need to conceal it; you can see it in the photographs of our yearbook — with long, thick auburn hair rising in a wave over my head, an elevated forehead, large eyes prone to show amusement, a strong nose and chin and a tight muscular build. As a matter of fact, I am a good deal the same to this day. Is that conceited? Well, conceit, no doubt, has been one of my problems. Mounty, at any rate, made no secret of his delight in my company; he insisted in my sixth-form year that I be a prefect in his dormitory, and he was a major influence in my decision to return to Saint Luke's as a master.

Was Mounty homosexual? I think he must have been, in all but the act. In his day it was not unusual for a man of even exclusively homosexual inclinations to live not only a life of absolute chastity, but to regard his secret lusts as temptations of the devil which it would be his soul's glory to resist to the end. The

Catholic priesthood must have known thousands of such, and the New England church schools have had their fair share. Not, of course, that temptation has always been resisted. We know about those altar boys, and what academy has not had to deal with masters who too much like to supervise students taking showers? But I have no doubt that Mounty has triumphed over every urge. Not only that, but that he regards as deserving of hellfire all those who have not.

After my graduation from Saint Luke's and during my four years at Harvard I constantly revisited the school, and Mounty, in whose dormitory I was welcome to a spare cubicle, would always urge me, when I left, to consider a teaching career. And how could I do better than the school we both loved? Doctor Dale, the veteran head, at the end of my senior year, no doubt influenced by Mounty, offered to employ me as a junior master, but I thought I had better see something of the world before closeting myself in academia, and I spent a fruitful year touring Europe as the tutor of a rich crippled boy. After that I worked for two years in a New York bank, at the end of the first of which I married my wonderful Anna, the bright young secretary of my boss. It was she who at last persuaded me to take up the offer of Doctor Dale. In many ways she carried on the job my mother had started.

"It's become very clear to me that you have that school in your heart," she told me. "I think we're kidding ourselves if we suppose anything else is likely to take its place. Not that you can't be a good enough banker. You're plenty smart enough to be a good enough anything. But I think you might be a great schoolteacher."

Anna was — and is — the best of sports. It couldn't have been easy for her to give up the prospect of the income that banking might bring me, for we had no capital of our own and one child already with another soon to follow. But she was, as always, a realist, and she knew me like a book. Her lovely sapphire eyes were settled firmly on the here and now. During the later period of the great innovations in the Saint Luke's routine — the admission of girls, the downgrading of the dead tongues, the widening of the student basis, the coming to terms with the sexual revolution — she never once indicated either approval or disapproval. Her constant nod to me gave me all the encouragement I was to have from my home: a simple "Yes, do it." If there were times when I wondered if she didn't accept change too readily, when I even caught myself for a horrid and quickly banished moment speculating on how she might have adapted herself to a fascist state, I was nonetheless deeply grateful for the silent, steady support she afforded me in my first major experiments.

Of course, no changes occurred in the school during my years of apprenticeship, when I was only a junior master and before I left to go to divinity school. But I studied every aspect of the school administration and was constantly mapping out in my mind how it could be restructured to fit into our rapidly changing century. I was very careful, however, to keep my ideas to myself, for the admirable but old-fashioned headmaster, though aging, showed no signs of releasing his firm grip on the academy he had so long ruled, and the senior faculty were blindly loyal to him. Mounty, for example, would have viewed with horror and scandalization the very idea of admitting girls to his male enclave. It was to you, my dear Robert, and to you alone that I imparted my views.

I don't know how you spotted me as one who would share your ideals. As Mrs. Browning might have put it, the chrism was on your head; on mine the dew, but death did not have to dig the level where these agreed. When I received a letter from Robert Chapin, chairman of the board of trustees, saying that he

wished to have a private talk with me on his next visit to the
school, I could hardly believe it until I found myself actually
strolling with you by the river that Sunday afternoon. I knew
that something had to be up, but I did not guess it was to be a
whole new world, and a brave one, too. That walk opened up
the correspondence in which we exchanged our ideas of what
the school might be and has become, thanks in largest part to
your ability to raise, and substantially contribute to, the funds
needed to effect our plans.

And then, some two years later, came that other walk with
you that I shall never forget, our stroll in the rose garden of the
garth by the chapel, that marked another turning point in my
life, when you informed me that if I was to have your backing for the headmastership that was to become vacant in four
years' time — on Doctor Dale's seventy-fifth birthday — I must
be ordained as an Episcopal priest.

You will remember how I argued with you. What did it matter that Saint Luke's in a hundred years had always had a clerical head? Was not evolution precisely what we had both agreed
upon? Would not the appointment of a layman be a ring-
ing statement of the coming elimination of outdated traditions?
But you were adamant. The old guard had to be won over, not
shocked. The very fact that a man of the cloth was advocating
new measures would make them more palatable. We would
have God on our side. And who was to say that He was not still
a potent ally?

Well, I was never quite sure when you were being cynical and
when you were not. You were fortunate in not suffering from
the bondage of a religious inheritance. The church to me was
my father's domain, and who was I to tread lightly on grounds
that had been sacred to him? But you were strongly backed up
by my Anna, who thoroughly agreed with you. She, of course,
wondered at first how we could afford the cost of divinity

school, with two children and the loss of my salary, but when she learned that you would more than make this up to us, she had no further doubts. Her "Yes, do it" this time was emphatic.

The only person who objected, when word got out of my plan to enroll in Harvard's divinity school, was Mounty, and his objection took more the form of a warning.

"I have only one question to put to you, dear boy. Would you be taking holy orders if it were not a prerequisite to a certain academic promotion?"

"What promotion do you mean?"

"Don't be coy with me, dear Guy. Do you suppose that your chats with Robert Chapin have gone unnoticed on this campus? If so, you are most naive. Why, I think even the school janitor must know that you are Chapin's candidate to succeed our revered head. Mind you, it is not that I disagree with our distinguished chairman. I think you would make a fine headmaster, and I would serve under you with pride. I think you have always been aware of my high opinion of you. But I am worried about this next step."

I hesitated. I was deeply touched by his confidence in me and felt that I had almost betrayed him in trying to conceal my relationship with the chairman. It was almost as if I could make it up to him by being strictly honest in responding to his inquiry.

"It's hard to know what I'd do in different circumstances."

"Is it? I should think it very simple. Take away Mr. Chapin and his offer. Would you still become a priest?"

I was about to take refuge in the excuse that I then could not afford three years in divinity school, but I decided this was not worthy of me. "No, I don't suppose I should."

Mounty at this became very grave. His thin lips almost disappeared as they tightened. "Then you have not a true vocation. Believe me, dear boy, you could become what you desire with-

out counterfeiting holy orders. There is nothing in the school
charter that requires a clerical head."

"Nothing but long tradition."

"A school rector could be appointed for sacred studies and
chapel services. He needn't be the headmaster or anything like
it. Trust me, Guy. I have studied these things. There was even a
time when *I* dreamt of such a promotion."

"But, Mounty," I argued, with some heat now, "hasn't teaching
always been a function of the church? Is it wrong, for example,
for a man to take orders because he wants to be a missionary?
Or a hospital chaplain? Or a teacher in a divinity school? Then
why not a teacher in a private boys' school? In a school named
for an evangelist?"

After a reflective silence Mounty slowly nodded. "Of course,
I've thought of that. You have a point there, it's perfectly true.
My only real concern — to be utterly frank — is *are* you a true
believer? You and I have discussed, it seems to me, everything in
the world *but* religion. I have sometimes even wondered if you
didn't consciously avoid the subject. That my own faith may
have been something that faintly embarrassed you. Something
that didn't quite fit into your modern world."

"*My* modern world?"

"Oh, yes, it's surely not mine. You are welcome to all of it,
dear boy."

I faced his question; there was no avoiding it. "I think I can
say that I'm a believer. In my own way."

This was followed by another pregnant pause. "There's only
one way, really. Just as there's only one truth and one life. But I
suppose I shall have to content myself with your answer. Just remember, my boy. I count on you. To the end."

And rising slowly he made his magisterial exit from my little
study in the schoolhouse. But he had confirmed an unease in my

soul — if that was where it was — which was to give me considerable trouble.

✻

The intellectual side of Harvard Divinity School, at any rate, interested me intensely. I couldn't read enough of the early church with its heresies and its councils, or of the subtleties of medieval theologians, or of the development of ritual, or of the reformation and the religious wars that followed. I could almost imagine myself becoming a scholar of the New Testament, seeking the dates and authorships of the Gospels and the Epistles. I had always been a history buff (it had been my major in college), and the story of the Christian religion was, after all, a principal part of the story of Western civilization. Where I had trouble was just where Mounty had warned me: in the matter of faith.

You, Robert, will be the first to whom this confession is made. I became a Christian priest without being a Christian. I not only found that I could not make myself believe in the divinity of Jesus — *that*, in these tolerant days might be forgiven even by my bishop — but I could not even believe that Jesus was a mortal inspired by God. Or for that matter, that he was even the true father of the Christian church.

Of course, these reflections are not novel, but they are, I hope anyway, novel, or at least rare, in an ordained minister. The man Jesus, it more and more seemed to me as I studied the synoptic Gospels, was something of a fanatic, a thaumaturgist who believed that the world was shortly coming to an end — in the lifetime, as he repeatedly warned people, of many then living — and that the only thing that now mattered was for them to prepare themselves for the terrible last judgment. This to me was the only valid explanation of why he urged his followers to have no care for the present, even for the closest family ties, or for the political order, no matter how unjust ("Render unto Caesar"), or for worldly possessions. What could anything matter to Jesus, or to anyone else really, if the day of judgment was truly at hand, but a speedy penitence and a hasty profession of faith?

Faith, always faith, that was what stuck in my craw. To Jesus the one true ticket to paradise was faith, blind faith, a faith that could move mountains, the simplest kind of faith, like that of little children whose supposed innocence made them closer to God. Surely only a confirmed bachelor could have believed in *their* innocence! And what of those who failed to attain this mental tabula rasa, this cringing submission to the divinity, this obliteration of self? Oh, they would be cast into hellfire, where they could express eternally with weeping and gnashing of teeth the individuality to which they had so blindly and stubbornly clung. It appalled me.

I did not overlook the fact that the Fourth Gospel never quotes Jesus as predicting the imminent end of the world. But I found reason for this in its having probably been written long enough after the crucifixion for the author to have come to suspect that Jesus must have been in error in this respect. It was now the job of the apostles, and in particular Saint Paul, to create a church that could deal with the world we must live in and not solely with the one that might follow our death.

All of which meant to me that I was entering a church that had been established by men whose judgment and leadership I was far from ready to admire. It seemed to me a church founded on fire and brimstone. Had not even Saint Paul started his career by stoning Stephen? Had not Henry VIII set up the Anglican faith in order to legitimate his adultery with "Nan Bullen, the whore"? And to do this had he not struck off the head of his chancellor, whom the Catholics have canonized? And had not even the canonized Thomas More busied himself while in office with the burning of Anabaptists?

Well perhaps, I reluctantly kept telling myself, faith *was* the only way, the only effective way at least, for the Church to rule. For look, today, when the spirit of faith has been succeeded by a tolerance which is only another name for indifference, how religion languishes, except in dark areas of the globe where it is violent, fanatical and nourished by civil war! But I was now resolving myself to allow it to languish. I decided that I must live my life and do my thing without it. Or thought I could. It was a hypocrite who ultimately took the priestly vows.

It was also a hypocrite whom you persuaded your board of trustees to name the successor to Doctor Dale. I was a welcome choice; hale and hearty and under forty, a known lover of the school, popular with boys and faculty, I was seen as one who would steer the school through the troubled waters of our age by making adjustments that would satisfy the modernists without too much riling the conservatives. But I was determined to use everything at my disposal, including the Church, to make Saint Luke's a leader in twentieth-century academic thinking.

I use the word "hypocrite" advisedly. I realized early that it would be detrimental to my projects to be totally candid with anyone, even with you, even with my dear Anna. For when, while still in divinity school, I started to confide in the latter my doubts about the role of Jesus in church history, she interrupted me firmly.

"That's something I don't want to hear anything about, Guy. I have not been married to you all these years without detecting that you have deep down somewhere in your psyche a streak of self-destruction. Keep it down. Way down. For if it ever really comes out, I may take the children and leave you."

Will you believe what next happened? That night, alone in our apartment (Anna had gone to her ailing mother for the weekend), I had an experience such as Henry James, Senior, father of the novelist and the philosopher, describes as a "vastation." It seemed to me that there was an invisible shape squatting in the room "raying out from his fetid personality influences fatal to life."

It didn't last. After a bad night I was myself again. And intellectually, of course, I could plainly see that the experience had been the result of a fevered imagination. But emotionally, I was convinced I had been visited by the devil. For what purpose? Was he with me or against me?

I pass over an account of the major school changes wrought in the first three years of my headmastership. You know them as well as I, having participated fully in every one of them and having so skillfully in each case "sold" it to your sometimes wavering trustees. What I wish to trace is the opposition led in the faculty largely by Mounty, who remained in constant communication with the retired head and with the more doubting members of the board. For it was in Mounty that I identified my occasionally revisiting squatting presence — that is, when I didn't identify it in myself. As I say, this was an emotional rather than a cerebral reaction, but emotions are real, too.

Mounty started his campaign of resistance moderately enough, with his reasoned arguments against our first major change: the admission of girls to the school. He came to my office to expound his views. We were still then on cordial terms.

"Have you stopped to consider, dear boy, that no civilization that deserves the name has ever tried to educate the sexes together at their age of maximum libidinous curiosity, i.e., the late teens?"

"What are you talking about, Mounty? Every high school in the country does that."

"In the morning or afternoon. In the classroom. Not boarding together under the same roof, away from their parents, twenty-four hours a day."

"But we're not planning to put them in the same dormitories."

"I suppose I should be thankful for *that*. But do you really suppose there are not nooks and crannies enough, not to mention the surrounding meadows and woodlands, to provide for ample carnal intercourse?"

"That is something, of course, that will require management."

"*Something!* The French, who never underestimate the young, used to lock their girls up in convents until they were of marriageable age."

"Yes, but that day is past, even in Spain. A bride doesn't have to be a virgin anymore."

"Does that mean she must be a tramp?"

"Oh, Mounty!"

"You'll see, my friend, you'll see. The cellars of this school will be brothels before you know it."

I have tried to laugh at Mounty's predictions, but you and I know, my dear Robert, that there *has* been sex in our cellars, in the woods, in the fields, by the river, perhaps everywhere — how do I know? And that I've done nothing about it. What could I? How could I say that sexual intercourse is wrong when the whole thrust of our society is simply to educate the young to engage in it safely? All I have really done is close my eyes to it. Yet I have had dreams, nightmares rather, when our lovely campus has taken on the flickering light and wild music of the Venusberg scene in *Tannhäuser* and when I have shocked the assembled barons of the Landgrave of Thuringia — the trustees no doubt of our revered academy — with obscene accounts of my stewardship! And even in the daytime, supposedly freed of dreams and fantasies, when I see couples strolling around the campus with arms around each other's neck, I sometimes feel a

Mounty impulse of revulsion. There is that squatting presence again!

My next clash with Mounty was a much sharper one. He had caught two boys in his dormitory in bed together, and he wanted them suspended, if not expelled. When I declined to take any action, he became very wroth.

"I suppose you cannot discipline boys for something that has come about through your own misguided policies."

"How do you deduce that?"

"Because, Headmaster" — he now used this English form of address to stress the new distance between us — "your introduction of girls to Saint Luke's has actually encouraged homosexuality. If that seems a paradox, let me explain. Take a boy who has developed sexually more slowly than his peers. He has no family, no older brothers or father to reassure him, only the daily, hourly presence of his contemporaries with their ignorant obsession with sex. Aren't you interested in girls, they keep hammering at him. If not, why not? Well, if you're not, you must be interested in boys! Stingy old Mother Nature gave us only two sexes. Choose! You've got to choose! They may not mind his being gay, but he must be something!"

"Well, maybe it's natural for him to be gay."

"But the decision shouldn't be thrust upon him before he's ready! He may get wedded to a habit which isn't his true destiny!"

"You don't think, then, Mounty, that homosexuality may be something that's decided by our genes?"

"That God put it there? I most certainly do not! If it's anyone's making, it's the devil's!"

It may have been ridiculous, but I started at the word "devil." I have always had to fight an almost nauseous disgust at the very concept of oral and anal sex; no amount of disciplined modern thought can quite eradicate it. And I recalled a visit I had made years before to the Escorial in Spain, when my guide had showed me in one of those vast bare courtyards the spot where buggering altar boys or young novitiates had been burned alive. How I could almost feel the flames licking at my skin!

I feared that if we went on with the subject, we might come too close to Mounty's own secret impulses and wound him, which was the last thing I wanted to do. So I left him vastly dissatisfied, and we had no further private conferences. I believe Mounty had given me up at this point and that from now on he was watching me balefully with the aim of catching me in an impeachable offense.

His opportunity, or at least what he regarded as such, came last winter, after a Sunday lunch, when I was leaving the great dining hall and passed the fifth-form table at which he always presided. He joined me suddenly and walked to the door at my side.

"Could I prevail upon you, Headmaster, to have a demitasse in my study? I have a matter of some gravity which I would like to discuss with you."

Nodding, I followed him up the stairway to the big, high-ceilinged study that formed, with its suite of bedroom and dressing room, the best apartment for a dormitory master that the school could boast. I rarely came to his study now and was impressed anew at how attractively it was decorated, thanks to his private means, with fine French chairs and settees, lovely Sèvres and Meissen in a huge glass breakfront, and bookcases packed with his collection of "firsts" and exquisite bindings. It must have taken all his strict discipline and the fact that his dormitory was made up of older and more discreet boys, selected by himself, that preserved his possessions on evenings when they all gathered there to be read to or listen to music. It was a bit much for a boys' school, but one could appreciate Mounty's sincere desire to expose his students to a wider culture than most of them had known.

He was very grave, as he poured me a cup of coffee from the pot on his hot plate. "At Communion this morning I found myself much agitated at the thought of this meeting. I was not in the right frame of mind to go to the altar, so I abstained."

"You don't mean that your thoughts were irreverent?" I asked with a smile.

There was no answering smile. "Well, *you* must tell me that. You're the priest. I was wondering if our Lord, who knows all, would approve of the Saint Luke's you have forged."

"Forged?"

"Surely it is your own creation. Surely it cannot be *His*."

"The sea is His and He made it, and His hands prepared the dry land."

"But fornications and unnatural couplings in the student body? His name taken in vain all around the campus? Non-Christians excused from divine service?"

I had not realized the fullness of my resentment of his opposition. I had worried too much about my own neurotic doubts as to my own inspiration. But now, as I viewed his fat, bland countenance so firmly closed to all reason and sense, I felt my throat thicken with distaste. For a minute my voice seemed strangled, but when I found it, it had a clear sarcastic ring.

"How would Christ think of *you*, Mounty? You know what He said about the rich man and the needle's eye."

"Very well. But I have dedicated myself and my possessions to His service. Which brings me to the point. Rose Chisolm. The beautiful sixth-former who left school to have an operation and was gone six weeks, has returned more bold and buoyant than ever. Do you know the nature of her operation?"

"I believe her father told me it was an appendectomy. With a difficult aftermath."

"It was an abortion. We are not sure who the father of the foetus was. I believe there were several candidates among our manly sixth-formers, trained in the school of Guy Lansing."

I knew now that the crisis had come. *My* crisis. Whatever *that* was. And I knew at once, with a strange conviction, just what I should do. Not why. I did *not* know why. That was what was so strange about it. And why I stalled for a moment.

"How do you know that?"

"You will recall that she has a younger brother in the third form. Her parents were apparently indiscreet enough to make him promise to be silent. Naturally, he couldn't sit on a story as hot as that. If the whole school doesn't know by now, tomorrow it will."

"And what do you propose that I should do about this?"

Mounty stared. "Well, I didn't think there would be much question even in *your* mind. Obviously, the girl must be expelled."

I rose. "Not while I'm headmaster."

Mounty rose to face me. "You will do nothing about it. *Nothing?*"

"Nothing at all. I was aware of her condition and how she planned to take care of it. And I told her she could come back to school."

I had the immediate feeling that Mounty didn't believe me. And in the months of academic turmoil that followed I think he was the only one who didn't. Except Anna when I told her. She believed me right away; she knew that I was quite capable of lying to bring on my own dismissal. And, of course, Mounty never let on to his own suspicions; he was too anxious to procure my ouster.

"You amaze even *me!*" he gasped now.

"Does it never strike you, Mounty, that morality for most people in our world is largely limited to sexual relations? They take for granted that you mustn't commit violent crimes like murder or robbery. And perjury, cheating, preferring oneself to one's friends or family, getting the better of the next guy in life, are all venial faults too common not to be forgiven. It's only sex that gets the scandal and the headlines. Well, I wonder if they haven't got it just the wrong way around. The only thing that makes a sexual act wicked is someone else's jealousy, and isn't jealousy a sin?"

Mounty closed his eyes as if in actual pain. When he spoke, his tone was gentle. "Please go now, Guy," he said, calling me that for the first time in more than a year. "You are not only not a priest. You are a pagan."

And that was it. That was all. The rest of the story must be only too engraved on your memory: Mounty's appeal to the trustees, the formation of a committee to examine my conduct of the school, the committee's four-to-three recommendation that I be asked to resign and the board's ultimate rejection of this and its vote of confidence in myself. Of course, without your ardent support I would have been lost.

Anna has left me. I hope it is only temporary and that, when she has thought things over, she will come back. She walked out on me when she learned I had made up the story that I had known all along about the Chisolm girl going home for an abortion. She claimed that this was an act of gratuitous self-destruction and that I had not cared that I was destroying my home as well. She would not see that I was merely being consistent, that my conduct would have been the same if I *had* known. The board's vote of confidence may change her mind, but I can't be sure.

I suppose I am perilously near the position of not knowing what is the best way to train the young in our day. If I am to continue at Saint Luke's, however, it will be to go on as I have been going, but, in all frankness, that is for lack of a better idea. I don't think I believe in either God or the devil, but I seem to live in constant fear of both. My future is in your hands.

Guy Lansing

❀

Written on the bottom is this note in the chairman's hand: "I'll tell him he needs a holiday and that I do not recommend the trip to the Holy Land that headmasters used to take a century ago. His post will be waiting for him on his return. And I'll speak to Anna."

The Facts of Fiction

FLORA HASKELL'S most vivid and terrible memory was of a fine spring Sunday morning in the early 1890s, when she was nine years old and walking down Fifth Avenue from Fifty-seventh Street after church, between her grandmother Haskell and her maiden aunt Vicky, and saw approaching them, on the arm of a tall man in a high hat and frock coat, her mother, her own darling pretty mother, arrayed in soft furs and wearing the most exquisite little red velvet hat. Her mother, for some weeks now, had been unaccountably missing from home, or on what had been unconvincingly described by Daddy as "a trip abroad for her health," and it was presumably this absence, apparently not destined to be brief, which had brought about Flora's and Daddy's removal, and with all their wardrobe, too, to Granny Haskell's commodious but gloomy brownstone.

"But there she is!" Flora shrieked. "She's not abroad at all. There's Mummie!"

And at the same time she saw her mother stop and throw her arms out with a welcoming smile.

"Flora, sweetheart, come to me!"

But then something dreadful — yet, curiously enough, not altogether unanticipated — happened. Both her grandmother and her aunt clutched her and pulled her away. It was not, Flora remembered afterwards, so much what was called the "cut direct"; it was rather as if they were desperately dragging her away from the perilous edge of a beetling cliff. What the old lady and her ordinarily gentle maiden daughter appeared to be suffering from was a fit of panic, as if getting any closer to the lovely lady in the red hat would actually expose all three of them to some lethal disease.

Flora was about to struggle in earnest from the tight grasp of her relatives when she saw her mother grab the arm of the tall gentleman and hurry him away, as if, at all costs, to terminate an unseemly scene.

"You see, dear child, your mother herself doesn't want to talk to you," Flora's grandmother somewhat breathlessly explained as she and Aunt Vicky dragged the child on towards home. "She doesn't want us. She has taken her leave of us. We must let her go, dear. I know it's hard, but we must let her go. She chose it that way. She chose to leave your father and you."

"But, Granny, she stretched out her arms to me!"

"And pulled them back fast enough. Didn't you see that?"

That was the note that Granny and Aunt Vicky consistently took henceforth: that Flora's mother had preferred the company of the tall gentleman to that of her own family. Flora could privately understand her preferring the tall gentleman's company to that of her father, a ramrod of a man who, in the rare moments when he noticed his daughter at all, boomed at her with a crudely manufactured cheeriness. He, unlike his mother and sister, never mentioned his wife at all; he was a man of silences, but his silences were usually condemnatory, and he had a way at breakfast (the only meal Flora shared with him, indeed the only time of the day when she saw him at all) of making the egg that he neatly decapitated or the newspaper in which he was absorbed or the coffee that he noisily drank (there *was* noise there) express his sense of the utter irrelevance of other human beings to the strict ritual of his existence.

In any case it was abundantly clear to Flora that her mother's conduct, whatever its details — and they were by no means clear — was considered reprehensible by all around her, so bad indeed that it was never mentioned by even the cattiest girls at her school, though she was painfully aware that they giggled and sneered out of earshot. But not out of sight. Oh, no, they knew that she knew what they were whispering about!

Her refuge was in the old companion of her loneliness: her scribbling. She covered little white squares of paper with the tales of her imagination. Now she wrote one about a little girl whose mother had gone away. The girl didn't know at first why her mother had gone away. But one day she saw her mother approaching her, down a street, on the arm of a tall dark gentleman. Her mother paused and smiled at her. But the little girl leaned down to pick up a stone and shy it at her mother. It struck her on the lips, and the little girl saw her raise a hand to wipe the blood away. But her mother did not frown or look angry or even look surprised. She understood. Oh, yes, she understood!

Life was very quiet for an only child in Granny Haskell's brownstone amid the dark, heavy curtains, the bronzes of animals slaughtering or being slaughtered (a splendid stag overwhelmed by wolves was Flora's especial horror), the cluttered furniture, the closely hung, unlit landscapes and seascapes and carousing cavaliers. Its denizens, Granny and Aunt Vicky and four ancient maids, contributed to the feminine atmosphere of silence and discretion; the only masculine note was in Daddy's inviolable study with its dark unread sets of classics and its decanters of whiskey and cognac and in his bedroom with its grim old four-poster and the monogrammed brushes and combs drawn up like soldiers on his dresser. But the isolation of the male theme made a different point to Flora. To her there was little but bluster in Daddy's big nose and constant throat clearing, in the way he never awaited an answer to his perfunctory questions, in the dead gleam of his eyes through the glittering pince-nez. It was evident even to a child, particularly to an observant child, that her sweet, low-voiced valetudinarian grandmother gave the only orders that mattered to the obsequious household, gently articulated though the orders might be. For all her seeming passivity Granny might have been a Catherine de Medici with oubliettes at her disposal!

Granny's real function seemed to be to keep the world at bay; wasn't there safety behind the walls of the brownstone, safety from the streets outside into which her mother had disappeared? Flora went to few places beyond the heavy glass grilled front door: to school, of course, Miss Pyne's Classes, a few blocks away, to which she walked accompanied by a maid or by her aunt, and to the nearby homes of such of her classmates with whom she formed mild attachments, and to such amusements as a play appropriate for children or to the circus. Flora read about violence, about passion and romance, about wars and polar expeditions in books and magazines, where such things seemed properly to belong, and she continued to write stories, mostly for herself, though she did have a couple printed in the school quarterly magazine, and she talked about boys and love with one or two of her closer friends. But she continued to regard reality — or at least reality insofar as it was safety from a world of disappearing mothers — as the temperate zone created by Aunt Vicky, where relations between nice men and women were treated with blinking eyes and little screams of laughter, where strangers were apt to be unclean and never to be spoken to and the poor were poor because they drank.

But what would happen to it all when Granny died, an even-

tuality to which Granny herself did not hesitate, rather compla-
cently, to allude? Would Aunt Vicky and the old servants and
Daddy himself not disappear in a clap of thunder like Kundry's
castle in the long opera that Flora had to sit through every
Easter?

When she finished school, she "came out," but not much
more than by the tip of her nose, in a series of afternoon tea parties at home, a way of doing it already hopelessly old-fashioned
and only a little better than not doing it at all. But the Haskells
were old New York; they knew everybody they were supposed
to know, and the mothers of eligible young men were apt to suggest that at least one of old Mrs. Haskell's afternoons be attended. Flora was perfectly satisfied; she had no wish to play
other than a modest role in society. She hoped to get through her
debutante year, as Aunt Vicky always put things, "without anything terrible happening." And she was by no means inattentive
to the young men who came to the house. She had no wish to become in the long future for her father what Aunt Vicky was to
Granny.

Among the visitors was one who came to all her teas and
continued thereafter to call on Granny's "Sunday afternoons."
Though he was certainly not very young, somewhere between
thirty-five and forty, he was excellent company. Henry Stevens
was short and inclined to be chubby, though this impression was
moderated by his thick curly blond hair and large blue eyes,
which seemed always to express amusement. Indeed, everything about him exuded good humor. He made fun of the
world, sometimes genially, sometimes with the salt of malice,
and he was never tedious. He dressed well, though a bit loudly;
his silk ties and large handkerchieves were riots of color; his
black boots gleamed; he twirled a walking stick with a gold
handle. Yet he was reputed to be one of the able managers of the
great furniture store that his late father had founded and that

he and his staider and soberer two older brothers ran. Henry, however, unlike most American businessmen, left the shop quite behind him when he went into society. It might have been that he sensed that "retail" business still curled an occasional lip in Mayfair, or it might have been simply that he enjoyed playing the role of the clown — a clown who, like Rigoletto, might conceal a stiletto behind his jokes.

On his sixth visit he led Flora to a settee in a window embrasure and asked her to marry him. The proposal had not been preceded by even a formal profession of affection.

"I think we are both, my dear, acquainted with the expected ritual of mating in our brownstone metropolis. I credit you with too much sense to sit placidly by while I spread my tail feathers and crow or even challenge other young men to personal combat. I tell you frankly that you suit me exactly. I greatly admire your quiet good looks, your unaffected manners and the skillful play of your mind. I venture to suppose that we would be a thoroughly congenial couple. Your family certainly approve of me; otherwise my visits would have been discouraged. Of course, I realize that the shopkeeping Stevenses are not on a social par with the colonial Haskells, but you and I know that a wholesale bank account covers a multitude of retail sins. Or to put it in the words Saint-Simon quotes of Madame de Grignan when her son married a *nouveau riche* heiress: 'Old fields need manuring.'"

Flora was a bit bewildered but not greatly upset by the loud burst of laughter with which he capped this declaration. Was it possibly the answer to everything? Jokes? She supposed there could be worse things.

"But you haven't spoken of your *feelings*, Mr. Stevens. You haven't said anything about your heart."

"Nor have I asked you about yours. Grant me that. Do you suppose that means I don't have one? I have as big a one as any person in this room." He cast a rather superior glance about the chamber. "And I'll take you away from all this! I'll give you a Beaux-Arts mansion as florid and vulgar as the oldest Knicker-bocker family could want." Oh, that laugh! "And you could al-ways boast that you had kept an old bachelor from being the last leaf on the tree!"

Yet she was touched; yes, she was touched. And there were certainly a lot of things worse than being Mrs. Henry Stevens. She told him, of course, that she would have to think it over, and he jumped up to take his leave. Too quickly. But if she was going to take him, she would certainly have to take him as he was. She could perfectly see that nothing was ever going to change Henry Stevens.

When he came back the following Sunday and the next, he did not press her for an answer, or even once refer to his pro-posal. But he led her again to the window embrasure to discuss himself and his family as if to give her the full disclosure in a brochure of what to expect as a Stevens in-law. The only thing about which he was consistently serious, she gathered, was his family.

There were six of them, three brothers and three sisters, chil-dren of the late founder of the emporium, a Scottish immigrant, who had formed a united front in their assault on old New York. All had married, and married well, but Henry. Mrs. Astor has been once quoted as saying: "Just because we walk on their carpets doesn't mean we must dine at their tables," but she had been long since won around, and the oldest sister, Abby Suy-dam, was now listed by Ward McAllister in his Four Hundred. After all, they were convivial, good-mannered and respectable; the battle had not been a hard one.

If he did not speak of his proposal to Flora, he did to his family, and its *doyenne*, Abby Suydam, a rather sweeping, ample-bosomed presence, as constantly smiling as her younger brother, called on Granny Haskell to emphasize the vociferous support of all the Stevenses.

Mrs. Haskell that night took the unusual step of going to her granddaughter's bedroom on the fourth floor. Flora always retired there when she wished to record the day's events in the journal, half fact and half fiction, which she devotedly kept. Seated in the chair by the girl's writing table Mrs. Haskell asked her earnestly if she had decided to accept Henry Stevens.

"Do you think I should?" Flora asked, almost with curiosity.

"You're not in love, then, my dear?"

"I'm not sure. Shouldn't I be?"

"Sure? Not necessarily. Sometimes one is without being sure. Sometimes love comes after marriage, or rather with it. Certainly Mr. Stevens is sure."

"What makes you think that?"

"Well, his sister seemed very sure of it."

"I guess he wants to be."

"He wants to be married. Of course, one sees that. Most men do. They want to settle down. They want to have a family. It's expected of them. Your grandfather was that way. His mother used to hound him with the cry 'I want grandchildren!' Isn't that perfectly natural? What's wrong with it?"

"Nothing. But is it a sufficient reason for *me* to marry him? I'm asking you seriously, Granny. I don't know. And obviously you think I should. Please tell me why."

Mrs. Haskell sighed. It was a deep sigh. "I see I must be candid with you, my dear. Totally candid. I know your father will never tell you, and your aunt Vicky knows nothing about it, so it's up to me. You and I must face facts."

"I'm trying to do that, Granny."

"Good. Then I start by pointing out that you are by no means what is called an heiress."

THE FACTS OF FICTION

"I never thought I was."

"Listen to me, dear. You've had every reason to believe you would ultimately be left a comfortable maintenance. And so indeed it should have been. But unhappily your father, who has been in charge of my finances, has not had what our French friends call *la main heureuse*. In fact his uncertain judgment has so impaired my capital that I shall be constrained to leave every penny that I have to your poor aunt if she is to maintain her life with any decency. And that is why my one wish is to see you properly settled before I depart this life."

Flora promised that whatever answer she should give her suitor would be very carefully considered, and then she accompanied the old lady down to her own bedroom and helped her to prepare for the night. She was in a hurry to get back to her writing table. It gave her an odd little thrill that she should have so exactly diagnosed the precarious fortifications of the Haskell brownstone. There was her father chug-a-rumming away, acting the part of the never-to-be-questioned, understandably preoccupied man of affairs surrounded by useless withered virgins and a senescent mother and all the while devouring their slender competence! A whole novel in itself, or certainly a novella! And Granny seeing it all too late, having to face on the brink of the grave the foolish confidence she had given to a male peacock!

But in the meanwhile she had better make sure of Henry Stevens before she was swept onto the street by the demolition team. In that Beaux-Arts mansion that he had promised her, and which would be quite as ugly and showy as *he* and not she would wish — oh, yes, she quite saw *that* — she might be quite content, writing beautiful, beautiful tales. She could hardly wait for the next Sunday to accept him. Had she not better write him a note? Or would that seem too eager? And yet, if Granny died that night, and it turned out that she was now not only a girl with a disgraced mother but a penniless girl with a disgraced mother, might the united Stevenses not suddenly change course? After all, how socially secure were they?

But the following Sunday, before Henry arrived, Flora had a talk in the same window embrasure with her second cousin, Albert Allen, a tall, bald, thin, formal bachelor of some forty years who acted as Granny's lawyer and was reputed to be wise, exact and kind. He had always taken a particular interest in Flora, because, she suspected, of her rather forlorn position in her grandmother's (his aunt's) household, and he considered his position as family counsel as justifying, indeed as requiring, what so discreet a person as himself would ordinarily deem a personal intrusion.

"If I thought you were deeply involved emotionally with Mr. Stevens, I would hold my tongue. But I have talked quite candidly with Aunt Harriet. She thinks a marriage with him a politic course for you. As you have received advice from one member of the family, I see no reason it should not be balanced with another's, and I have told her so, and she has agreed, however reluctantly. I think you can do better than Mr. Stevens. I think you should marry for love."

"I didn't know you were such a romantic, Albert."

"I have no claim to be one. I consider myself a realist. One who faces the facts of happiness in life. And unhappiness."

"And you don't think Henry Stevens loves me."

"On the contrary, I daresay Henry Stevens loves you as much as a man like Henry Stevens will ever love anybody. It's your feeling, or lack thereof, that I'm considering."

"But don't you think he'll make me a good husband?"

Albert considered this. "As the world views it, yes. His family are like brownstone fronts. The appearance may not be beautiful, but it's beyond reproach. The Stevenses represent the world.

Perhaps the best of the world. But it's still the world. And only the world."

"You think they have no soul?"

"I think *you* have one."

"But such a weak one. Oh, Albert, you're a man and can stand on your own two feet. But I'm full of fears and apprehensions. I'm such a coward!"

"What are you afraid of?"

"That Granny will die and leave me penniless. She's told me about Daddy and his poor management. You must know all that."

"Yes, but you won't be destitute. There's a family fund of which I'm trustee. It will always pay for necessities. You don't have to be rich, my dear, to be happy."

"But I want much more than necessities, Albert! I want to be secure. I want to be safe. I want a family around me to protect me. I don't want to be cast out in the world like my mother!"

"Your mother is not cast out. She's living quite comfortably in Paris."

"Well, you know what I mean. Nobody speaks of her. Nobody here, anyway. And anyway it's time I had a husband. Before anything happens to Granny. A man, of course, doesn't have to marry. Nobody calls you an old maid."

"I'm not so sure of that. But why do you care what people call you? You don't have to marry at all if you don't wish."

"What would I do then?"

"You could write, couldn't you? Isn't that what you most like to work at?"

"It's not my work. It's my life!"

His eyes flickered with a sudden interest. "How you say that! I wonder if it doesn't explain."

"Explain what?"

"Why you're so indifferent to what most girls dream of."

"And what's that? A great romance?"

"Don't sneer at it. It may surprise you. And if it comes unexpectedly, it had much better come to Miss Haskell than to Mrs. Stevens."

"Ah, now you're warning me," she exclaimed with a laugh. "You don't want me to end up like Anna Karenina under a train!"

"Well, I don't think you'd ever come to *that*," he murmured and then rose to take his leave. He had fulfilled his duty.

In the first three years of her marriage Flora had often the occasion to reflect that she had been more correct about her own needs and capacities than her cousin Albert. But she in no way blamed him for this. How could he, without having experienced the loneliness and apprehensions of her childhood, and being a male to boot, possibly assess the inordinate and continuing relief that the solid backing of so united a clan as the Stevenses furnished her? They were always *there:* to laugh with her, to swap stories with her, to play games with her, to pay her pretty compliments and to accept them from her. There was a gay, an even frivolous side to their kindness and partiality, but the comforting feeling was always with her that at the first snicker of hostility from an outsider, at a party, on the beach in Southampton, on a club terrace, in a plant-crammed conservatory, they would at once form a united cohort to defend her, like a circle of closely arrayed yaks lowering their formidable horns to keep off a pack of snarling but frustrated wolves. The Stevenses lived only a few blocks from one another in town and occupied a string of shingle cottages in the Hamptons; the women shopped together and drove out together and constantly called on one another, but at any social gathering — and they were incessantly gregarious — they drew apart and dedicated themselves to the company. Yet even there they kept a wary eye alert for any of the tribe in trouble: a maid "stuck" on the dance floor, a brother in the grip of a deadly bore, a nephew inclined to drink more than was good for him.

Henry as a husband was pretty much what he had been as a beau: affable, jokey, elaborately considerate in small matters, devoted to his business in daytime and to dinner parties at night, a relayer of spicy gossip and a devoted follower of the latest fashion, with the habit of pampering the little boy she had borne him after their first year together.

More intimately, he had been, at least at first, a perfunctory but methodical Saturday-night lover who seemed to regard his performance as a kind of weekly hygienic calisthenics. And even this he largely dropped after the birth of their boy which seemed to have been the real purpose of their bedtime encounters. She sometimes wondered what he had done in this respect as a bachelor, but her curiosity was mild. After all, he was easy to live with. Clearly, he had yielded to family pressure in taking a wife. He had wanted to be a respectable married man. Well, had she not wanted to be a respectable married woman? Her mother's daughter did not need to be told that there were worse things.

And she had time to write, all morning, every morning! The little Beaux-Arts house with the high, green iron roof and the bull's-eye windows was run jointly by the butler and Henry, who were delighted not to be interfered with. Henry indeed applauded her literary habit and boasted of it to the family, but neither he nor any of them ever asked to see a sample. They were not great readers, and Flora's "little hobby" probably struck them as a harmless game of solitaire.

She had tried her hand at novellas, usually based on her father, a fatuous ass chained in a wretched marriage to a romantically inclined wife, but she found that she did not have enough knowledge of her mother's life to make the stories real, and she turned now to a subject that she had more to hand: the Stevenses. Once started, her novel seemed almost to write itself. Her pencil flew over the yellow pads, and each day by lunchtime she had a neat little pile of sheets. And reading them over was not painful as with the novellas; it was joy. It was *joy*!

Her hero was modeled along the lines of her cousin Albert, converted from a lawyer to a famous surgeon. He was cool, aloof, superior, detached from the noisy world that acclaimed him. But whereas Albert, so far as she knew, was chaste, his counterpart in her tale was entangled in an endlessly protracted affair with a beautiful but heartless society lady, married to a complacent spouse, and bored, disillusioned, rotten to the core. It was one of those liaisons that have become as accepted by society as a dull marriage. But then the doctor meets and falls passionately in love with the heroine, Leonora, a lonely, desperate soul, trapped in a loveless marriage and held in the grip of her husband's tightly organized family of social climbers. And Leonora's husband? Ah, how author Flora *saw* him! He was Henry Stevens to the life, but with a sinister streak of cruelty, sarcastic, brilliant, a bit of a sadist. The doctor wishes to abandon his society practice and flee with his new inamorata to a Pacific island where he hopes to redeem his soul by curing the patients of a leper colony. She is unwilling to abandon her infant son, but her husband unexpectedly frees her by divorcing her publicly for an adultery of which she has not yet been guilty, and with a clear conscience she goes off with the doctor to the island where both die of leprosy but die happy.

There were moments when she wondered if her plot did not verge on the melodramatic, but the characters seemed to have come alive and to have taken the story, so to speak, between their own teeth. She had the feeling that the pace of the novel had asserted its own control over her material, and she could only hope that, as in *Jane Eyre*, its sensational aspects would form a fitting accompaniment to the central passion of her plot.

So greatly had writing been a solitary solace in her life that she had given little thought to publication as she turned out her chapters. But when publication came to her, it was as swift and easy as it was normally slow and painful to beginners. For among the constant diners-out in the fashionable world that she and Henry frequented was the friendly, beaming, expansive figure of the old dean of Manhattan publishers, Lucas Barnes, whose father and uncle had established the distinguished firm that he now headed. Barnes loved to expatiate on literary topics to young and attractive ladies at dinner parties, and the intense, dark-eyed little Mrs. Stevens who listened to him with such gratifying attention was a particular favorite. He might have been a little discouraged when he learned that she, alas, like so many, had a manuscript at home on which she would so *cherish* his advice — just his advice, really, or even that of one of his readers — but he was too gallant to refuse.

He *did* give it to a reader, but that reader gave it back to him with the enthusiastic recommendation that it be considered for immediate serialization in the firm's monthly magazine, and Barnes, reading it on the spot, saw it at once as a potential best seller.

Flora, ecstatic, decided that the time had come to show the manuscript to her husband. She couldn't be unaware that he might be startled at some of the resemblances of her characters to members of his family and even to himself, but she tried to argue herself into the hope that they might accept the fact that she had simply used them as starting points in creating a fancy world, like the plastic models that dressmakers use in their windows to show off their different apparels. And finally she attempted to buoy herself up with the heady feeling that publication might be exciting enough to make up for any dispute that she was fated to have with her in-laws.

Henry's effusive congratulations on the receipt of her news did not quite conceal his obvious astonishment, but he took her manuscript off to the office the next morning and promised to read it that very day. That night, however, he did not come home, but sent word that Flora was to meet him across the street at the house of his sister, Abby Suydam.

She found the two of them awaiting her in the parlor. Abby, whose large, usually cheerful features were now covered with what struck her sister-in-law as a kind of curtain of reserve, was seated stiffly in a bergère while Henry, standing by the fireplace and avoiding his wife's glance, stared into the grate.

"I of course have not had the time to read all of your book, Flora," Abby began, "but Henry has marked certain passages for me. Am I to understand that you plan to publish the novel as it stands?"

"Oh, exactly!"

Henry turned to face her. Joking men, she now saw, could be desperately serious when they *were* serious. Her husband's round cheeks seemed to lengthen as he stared at her. "Do you really mean that, Flora? Without changing a word?"

Flora felt strangely exhilarated. Was this the way saints felt before a Roman inquisition? "Without changing a word!" she repeated emphatically.

"But, Flora, my dear," Abby interjected, "you can't expose us like that! People will say we must have horribly mistreated you!"

"People will always say stupid things. My characters are purely fictional."

"I wonder if you can be really prepared to take the consequences of what you're planning to do." Henry's tone had become almost speculative.

"I daresay there are consequences for everything we do. But to what in particular do you refer?"

"To the simple fact that our united family, who have welcomed you and loved you and cared for you, will feel that you have shamelessly betrayed them."

The image that now flashed across the screen of Flora's mind was a drawing in her childhood copy of *Alice in Wonderland* of Alice turning her antagonists at the trial into pasteboard with the cry: "You're nothing but a pack of cards!" And that's what they were! A pack of cards! Hadn't they considered her writing a game of solitaire?

But what she said was: "If they want to take that attitude, I can't stop them."

"*Want* to!" Abby and her brother exchanged glances of consternation. Then Abby said abruptly to him: "Let me talk to Flora alone."

When Henry had left the room, and Flora noted how quickly he availed himself of the opportunity — the big things were always left to Abby — the latter's expression seemed to change more to surmise than disapproval.

"I don't understand you, Flora. You look complacent. Even smug. Are you actually *glad* to hurt us?"

"Oh, no, not at all. It's just that I think you're all foolish to be so hurt. By a book. Just a book."

"It's evidently more than just a book to you, dear."

"Well, I think it gives me relief. If that's the word."

"Relief from what?"

"Perhaps it's relief that I find I can stand on my own two feet."

"Against the family?"

"Not that. No, it's not that at all. I think it's that I've found that I can stand on my own two feet *without* the family."

"You can't mean that you want to leave us?"

"Oh, no, no, no. I want you all. And Henry, too, of course. I need you. But I don't want to need you too much."

"Too much for what?"

"Too much to be myself. Too much to be a writer."

Abby stared at her for a long moment and at last she nodded. "I guess I can see that. Well, let's call Henry back in. We'd better start putting our heads together on how best to face our brownstone world when your book hits them."

※

Flora's novel duly appeared in monthly installments and had a considerable success, though in New York it was largely a *succès de scandale*. People in the fashionable world read it as a *roman à clef*, but the Stevenses, united as usual, proclaimed it a work of genius and, happily acknowledging that the author had used them as models, lauded her talent as a great artist of caricature. "She's turned us all into monsters!" they cackled, as if she had organized a hugely successful costume ball in which they had all dressed up as the villains of famous novels and plays. Henry boasted that he had given her some valuable pointers on how to make the heroine's husband even more odious than she had originally intended. And when people grasped the family's party line, they accepted it and lost interest. After all, it was no fun unless the Stevenses were really hurt.

Flora was enchanted with her new fame. If there had been some negative reviews, there had been more that struck the note that the book was "hard to put down," and everyone opined that Flora Stevens was an author to watch.

"You see, I'll never end up as Anna Karenina," she told her cousin Albert triumphantly one Sunday afternoon at her grandmother's. He had been only wryly amused at the portrait of himself as the doctor. "I've got something in my life now that's far better than any Vronsky."

"You mean your novel?"

"I mean my writing. It's a joy that we artists mustn't boast about too much, because if the poor benighted folk who can never know it should ever find out how great it is, they might become discontented with their own little substitutes of love and passion."

"I think you're right, anyway, to keep it to yourself."

After his talk with her, Albert sat down for a minute beside her grandmother's chair. The old lady had been scandalized by Flora's novel.

"I can't understand the Stevenses saying they like it," she protested to her nephew. "In their position I should have been outraged."

"Oh, they know the value of teamwork. The whole thing has blown over already."

"But don't you think they *did* mind?"

"I think they've almost convinced themselves they didn't. No, it's not them, it's Flora I'm worried about."

"I suppose you're worried about what her next book will be. Could it be any worse?"

"You mean from the point of view of pillorying her acquaintances? Probably not. But when her novelty has worn off, the critics may start to call spades spades."

"Ah, you think she's no good? As a real writer, that is?"

"My dear aunt Harriet, she writes the most abysmal trash!"

"But if she sells, isn't that what she wants?"

"No! She fancies herself another Charlotte Brontë. And if she loses that faith in her star . . ."

Mrs. Haskell gaped as he paused. "She loses everything?"

He shrugged. "Well, I guess people don't jump under trains anymore."

"Good heavens, Albert, was there ever any danger of *that*?"

"There wasn't. But if she should ever have the bad luck to be persuaded that she *isn't* Charlotte Brontë, if she should ever have a glimpse of how atrociously bad a writer she is, and if she should then look at Henry and see what an ass she has married —"

"Albert! He's not that! You go too far."

"But not much too far, Aunt Harriet. Even you will have to concede that. And then if a Vronsky should appear on her scene, I for one should not answer for the consequences."

The old lady looked across the room to where her granddaughter was entertaining a circle of admirers, and a shrewd look suddenly flashed in her eye. "But nothing is ever going to persuade her she's not our great lady of letters. Just look at her, Albert!"

"I *am* looking at her, Aunt Harriet." And he was, taking in the simper of amiable condescension on Flora's countenance as she listened to a congratulating fan. "And, of course you may be right. She may live to be eighty, as confident of the immortality of her fatuous romances as the famous Ouida. But Flora has some bitter childhood memories, the kind that great novelists turn into masterpieces. One day she may be tempted to write her own story — *not* just that of the people around her — and then the difference between the grim truth and the lamentable style may become apparent even to her. She once let me see the notebook in which she inscribed her juvenilia. It had an eerie tale in it about a little girl who threw a stone at her mother and struck her on the mouth, causing her to bleed."

"Good heavens, let us hope she'll spare us *that* one!"

"Let us pray."

The Virginia Redbird

I sit here on my narrow front porch behind the loggia of fat round white Doric columns, so much grander than the modest red brick building that seems almost to huddle behind them as if embarrassed by so braying an introduction, and gaze placidly out over the big box on the drive (I like to tell visitors that it was planted by a gardener of George II who came over to work for our colonial governor) toward the distant line of the Blue Ridge Mountains in the late afternoon of a radiant autumn. And I feel that my own old age is peacefully in conjunction with the easeful demise of summer. The young law student from the university who has just left and who is kind enough to drive out from Charlottesville on Saturday afternoons to call on a lonely old lady has certainly a most un-Yankee appreciation of this shabby old place that I just manage to maintain with two darkies as old as their mistress, who were born in Peyton's Grove and expect to die here, but whom I can pay only with their board and keep.

The dear young man is a New Yorker and well-to-do; he brings me presents of wine and lovely fruits and the latest books in shiny dust jackets. He is entranced by my stories of the past and keeps urging me to "write them up." He likes to call me "Princess," using the title given to me by my late beloved husband, Peter Zokorov, rather than the simple "Zelina," by which

I am known to friends and relatives of all ages. And I rather like it, from him. The title that sounds pretentious to many Americans has a fairy-tale ring as he uses it; it seems to go with the beautiful faded quality of the sad old house and the unweeded garden and the green fields and the rich red mud of our Virginia countryside. Why shouldn't he have his dreams, poor young man, so soon, no doubt, to be caught up in our inevitable involvement in this terrible war that the beast Hitler has launched?

Were there not almost half a century between his age and mine, my two old darkies might think, as he always arrives bearing flowers, that he was courting me! He is bold enough to declare that he finds me still a great beauty. But I have learned a good deal about men, young and old, and I recognize in Frederick the idealistic and still innocent youth who finds an outlet for his romantic imagination in a woman too old to be a threat. And that's all right. Some men gain their sexual confidence later than others. Frederick, I feel sure, will not go the way of the sublime author of *Dorian Gray;* he will marry in his thirties some dear little girl, of deceptively docile appearance, who will dominate him completely and make him absurdly happy. God bless her! He has brought me needed diversion.

One of the books he gave me was the memoirs of my first husband's sister, Dorothy Doremus, *A Life on the Hudson*, about the rearing of herself and her orphaned siblings in the great old family homestead by that mighty river. She speaks briefly of the less than happy period of our relationship, and she pens an appreciation of my appearance but only of that. "When the Virginian beauty, Zelina Peyton, first hove into our sight, we were properly dazzled. She had the largest dark blue-green eyes, the largest thin black lashes, a glorious halo of lovely curled ash blond hair with a faint tint of red, the most delicately chiseled features and well-curved lips. She was indeed the siren that her admirers described. In the early days of her ill-fated marriage to my brother Adrian, she wrote me some letters that I regarded as lyrical. But discovering them recently in an old drawer and rereading them, I was put in mind of shriveled flowers."

It is easy to say that Dorothy, always a very plain woman and now a haggard old maid, hated me for a beauty that she would have sold her soul to acquire, but her animus is more than that. It has found its counterpart again and again in my life. People, both men and women, seem to have sought in my beauty — and, yes, let me call it that, at whatever risk of conceit, for it has been the central point of my story — some kind of ideal to sustain their faltering faith in a world constantly shadowed by sin and terror. And, of course, they haven't found it because it wasn't there. It wasn't ever meant to be there. But missing it, their admiration has too often soured into contempt.

I was born in Peyton's Grove only five years after Appomattox in a Virginia devastated by the war. My father, who was fifty when I was born, had been on General Lee's staff; twice severely wounded and prematurely aged, he spent his last years largely on this very porch where I am sitting, seeking solace, I always supposed, in his memories of a better day. But if he was nostalgic, he was not bitter. Mother, ten years younger, was. Her hatred of the Yankee was undying, her resentment of our new poverty without remittance. And she never faltered in her resolution to regain her old position. She took an almost fierce pride in my looks: "You'll get it all back!" she would mutter, half to herself, but also half to me. Indeed, it was almost as if she were opening the initial campaign of a new civil war when she sent me to New York for a visit of indefinite duration to a cousin of hers who had married a rich northern railroad man. The match had originally been deplored by the assembled Peytons, but it was now seen in a different light. The train that took me from Richmond to Manhattan might have been a Trojan horse. Yet I carried no such threat in my heart. New York to me was a splendid adventure. I was not going to waste my life waving the bloody shirt.

Poor Mother! If she could see me now, back in our adored but tattered homestead, she would find her prophecy sadly unfulfilled. And yet at the time of her death, when Adrian and I were on our honeymoon in Rome, she had every reason to believe it was about to come true. There was I, the radiant guest of honor at a garden party at the American embassy, the newly wed bride of the handsome, dashing and rich Adrian Doremus, author of the international best seller, *Madame*. How that moment comes back to me! I feel my eyes fill with sudden burning tears as I lower the glass of champagne that I have just raised to my lips. Because before me, on the carved marble branch of the laurel tree into which a sculpted Daphne is depicted turning, has alit a scarlet bird.

"What is that bird?" asked an Italian lady who had followed my fixed stare. "I don't think I've ever seen one before."

"Why, it's a cardinal!" exclaimed the ambassadress. "I didn't know there were any in Rome."

This was followed by a ripple of laughter from the group.

"No, she means it's an American bird!" I cried in a voice that startled everyone. "At home we call it the Virginia redbird. And it always appears when someone in my family has died!"

I hurried to my husband's side, and he took me hastily back to our hotel, where I found the cable announcing my mother's demise. The redbird did not appear when my beloved Peter Zokorov died; it comes only for one of our blood.

The cousin in New York to whom Mother sent me when I was twenty, Maud Stillman, was a kindly, gushing, still pretty widow of fifty-some years, who had not only not lost but amplified her southern accent and loquacity and who inhabited a tall, narrow marble-fronted mansion on Fifth Avenue whose fifth story sprouted unexpectedly into the Porch of the Maidens and where she gave parties for socialites whom she hoped enjoyed them half as much as she did. Her two daughters had already been successfully married off, and she was pining for a substitute on whom to lavish her residual powers of promotion. I fitted her bill to a tee.

The Gay Nineties was a period on both sides of the Atlantic when a cult of female pulchritude flourished. Albums of famous beauties enjoyed a brisk sale, and postcards of such celebrated "stunners" as Lillie Langtry and Lillian Russell were displayed in cigar stores. Society loves to indulge in "rages," however briefly, and I, for a season at least, was clasped to the big, stifling, diamond-studded bosom of the Four Hundred.

It was an unreal time, and I felt unreal. Yet I enjoyed the frothy adulation that engulfed me. I found charm in the city, even in the endless rows of chocolate facades made of a stone that Edith Wharton has described as the most hideous ever quarried. I found the houses simple and reassuring, so unlike their inhabitants, besides which their excessive sobriety was being attenuated by the showy new Renaissance palaces of Stanford White and Richard Morris Hunt. And my new friends seemed a curious but not unlively mixture of that same simplicity and ostentation. They were always dressing up for something; amusement had become a kind of public duty with a whole new code of rules and regulations. It was no coincidence that the favorite entertainment of the day was the fancy dress party. We were always putting something on to *look* like someone we weren't. Usually a king or a queen, or at least a duke or a duchess. We were a kind of caricature of a European court. It was all rather fun — at first.

That Cousin Maud was bent on arranging a great marriage for me was evident to all, and the fact that I had no dowry (her late husband had sagely left his fortune in trust) was not the stumbling block that it would have been abroad, where the sons of noble families were frequently bust. The heirs of Manhattan, on the contrary, were apt to be so rich that further endowment would have been idle, and a young Vanderbilt or Astor could afford to be more interested in beauty than in bankrolls. And as for family ... well, when Cousin Maud had let it be bruited about town that General Lee had been my godfather and the marquis de Lafayette my father's, no further questions were asked. The cards of eager and eligible bachelors filled the silver platter in her front hall.

The most eligible of all, and the one whose offer I accepted at the end of my year's visit in New York, was Adrian Doremus. He was indeed the beau of beaux: tall, handsome, superbly if a trifle flashily clad, with a lustrous pearl on his cravat and large sapphire cuff links, possessed of a high brow, a marble chin, black staring eyes and a backward sweep of long dark hair. He came of an old Hudson family with a sprinkling of new money from the distaff side, and he was the author of a best-selling, ultraromantic historical novel about the tragic love affair between the Sun King and his enchanting English sister-in-law. He spoke in a high, fluty voice that demanded the attention of all present to harken to his extreme views and even to challenge any male who dared to snicker to a personal encounter that the latter might well lose.

At the reception at Cousin Maud's, where I first met him, he led me, in a lordly fashion, to a corner where we could chat, as he put it, without "beastly interruptions."

"Tell me, divine Miss Peyton, how you, presumably raised amid all the beauty of the Old Dominion State, with traditions extending back to the dawn of colonial history, can bear to live surrounded by the horrors that garish decorators foist on the wives of burghers who have just made their first million."

"Are you referring to your hostess's parlor?"

"Is that what she calls this chamber? I might have taken it for the warehouse where she stored her first mistakes. You know: the things she bought before anyone told her about Elsie De Wolfe."

"You are very free with my poor cousin's taste."

"Your rich cousin, I should say. For these unscrupulous dealers, I am told, make fortunes out of their curious interpretations of what they imagine Madame de Pompadour to have liked." He glanced disdainfully about. "Is there *anything* quite so bad as their nineteenth-century conception of the French eighteenth?"

More amused than indignant, I had to admit he had a point. Every chair, every console, even every bracket in that room had a dead gilded air.

"Don't you even like the carpet?"

"Ah, I knew you had an eye!" he exclaimed. "The Aubusson is indeed a pearl. It's a curious thing about our burghers. They rarely go wrong in rugs. I suppose too many of them have Middle Eastern origins."

"In the south, Mr. Doremus, we were taught to speak less critically of the homes we visited."

"While within them, you mean. Away, no doubt, your tongues were freer. Much of my youth was spent in England, and I observed at house parties that even a duchess could be very frank about the little failings of her chatelaine. But I say nothing about the code under which you were raised, the product before my eyes being so fine. I bow to no one in my admiration for all your southern gentry. They were gallant in battle and noble in defeat. They represent the last stand of a true aristocracy."

"You sound, sir, as if you might almost regret the outcome of the war."

"Not that, never. My father fought in it, and two of my uncles perished at Gettysburg. And to this day the Doremuses barely nod to an old cousin who bought exemption from the draft. But

I recognize the price that we paid in the destruction of a grand old culture. Indeed, if I may risk a personal remark, I see it symbolized in the beauty that meets my eyes."

"But that makes me sound so dead and gone! And my mother tries to see in me a kind of southern rebirth!"

"Isn't it the same thing?"

Flattery can be delightful even when one knows it is that, and I was gratified to have this striking figure become a constant caller at the house whose interior he sniffed at. But I was never wholly taken in by him. I had imbibed some of the skepticism about men of my wise old black nurse, and there was precious little that I took for granted. I divined early that Adrian's contempt for society was simply a contempt for the vulgarity of the new rich in the gilded meeting places of Manhattan — at the opera, at Delmonico's, at the Waldorf-Astoria and up and down Fifth Avenue — rather than a condemnation of any economic injustice. An English marquis, possessed of thousands of acres and a palace in Mayfair, provided he had a smattering of cultivation and was a first-class shot, excited his warmest approval. Adrian was only too clearly what he stoutly maintained he was not: a snob. But the people he thought good enough for him were so small a group that it was easier to define him as a misanthrope.

Not indeed that he couldn't be charming. His very arrogance had a not unattractive side. A snob who likes *you* is on the road to forgiveness. And Adrian was able to convince a fair number of people that he cared for them more than he did. Why then did he bother? Because, for all his loudly proclaimed independence of soul, he wanted to be loved.

He took me to the theatre and to the opera and invited me up to the old mansion on the Hudson to meet his numerous brothers and sisters, all brilliant and individualistic like himself, but all seeming to recognize his natural leadership as the eldest and most individual of them all. I think I began to understand, even that early, that their loss of both parents and their having been raised by aunts and uncles, taking turns at the job and too often giving it up, had deprived them of the criticism and discipline that their unruly natures required. Adrian assumed proprietary airs about me; at social gatherings he would interrupt my conversation with another man as if it were only permissible to speak to me with his allowance.

Why didn't I object? I did, but not too much. Remember, he was considered the catch of New York. Not nearly as rich, to be sure, as an Astor or Vanderbilt, but brighter, more noticeable, more, in short, of a "personage," as Cousin Maud liked to put it, and possessed of a literary talent that the less sophisticated considered near genius.

Was I ever really in love with Adrian? I don't know. He dazzled me. I had never, in war-impoverished Virginia, imagined that I could have such a beau, and I couldn't help bearing in mind my mother's fierce conviction as to the true purpose and destiny of my own good looks. Might I not, as Mrs. Doremus, be able to refurbish our beloved Peyton's Grove and reestablish it as one of the loveliest estates in Virginia?

His proposal came on a Sunday afternoon when he took me riding in Central Park. I was glad of the occasion to show myself to best advantage; my father had trained me to be an accomplished equestrian, and I was sure that I looked better on horseback in the smart outfit that Cousin Maud had bought me than in her pompous parlor.

Adrian was riding slightly behind me when he made his offer. "It should hardly surprise you, my dear Zelina, to learn that I hope above all things to make you my wife."

It did not surprise me. I had rehearsed what I should say. But the actuality had some of the tension I had felt years before, taking my first part in a school play.

"What is it that makes you think I should suit you in such a role?"

"Oh, that's simple. The fact that you are the most beautiful woman in the world."

I nodded, as if considering a serious point. "And have you always wanted to marry the most beautiful woman in the world?"

"Of course! Browning said that a man's reach must exceed his grasp, or what's a heaven for? Well, it seems I've found that heaven. The only question is, can I get in?"

"Does it not bother you that beauty may be attended by every kind of fault?"

"Not beauty like yours! To me it is a guarantee of nobility of character."

"My goodness! But suppose I should lose my beauty. Should I lose you as well?"

"Never. I could live on the memory of it."

And it was on the strength of that answer that I decided to marry Adrian Doremus. His life, he assured me, had been the long pursuit of beauty — in art and in love.

🌸

When I went home to Peyton's Grove to prepare my widowed and now gravely ailing mother for the marriage that was to realize her dreams, I felt that I had tumbled from the fantasy world of a roseate cloud to a humbler but nonetheless welcome reality. Irritated, almost unendurably, by Mother's never-ending paeans of triumph, I took long solitary rides over the neighboring fields and pastures on the horse that Adrian had generously bought me and contemplated, at moments almost in near panic, the future to which I had perhaps rashly committed myself. For that generosity of Adrian's — now that I was away from him and could recollect and analyze the plans for our future that he had poured out to me and that I, in the daze that had followed our engagement, had only half listened to — turned out to be a rather limited commitment. There was not, apparently, nearly as much money as I had supposed, and it was all to be expended on maintaining a proper life style in London, where we were principally to reside, with occasional visits to New York. Oh, yes, there would be something left over to provide my mother with an allowance, but there could be no idea of any large-scale refurbishing of Peyton's Grove.

Could I back out? And break my poor sick mother's heart? It was unthinkable. I tried to picture the life that Adrian was offering me as a glamorous and exciting one. London, after all, would be better than New York. Society there admitted men of letters, artists, musicians, even actors. In New York, as Adrian had once put it: "If Emile Zola had called at Mrs. Astor's, he would have been sent to the service entrance."

Adrian and all his siblings followed me to Virginia in a month's time, and we were married in the little church where my parents and grandparents had been married before me.

And indeed London *was* amusing, at first, when we moved into our big white rented house in Belgravia, only weeks after my mother's death. As soon as my mourning was over — and Adrian cut it very short, arguing that nobody in London would be aware that I even *had* a mother — we began going to big parties. The Doremuses had connections in exalted circles, and we were asked everywhere. I may as well put it flatly that, for one season at least, I was the "rage" of the town, taken up by two great duchesses and toasted at every table. The Prince of Wales demanded that I be presented to him, and I was the subject of a full-page portrait-photograph in a popular monthly.

Adrian interrupted our social whirl briefly to take me over to Paris to be painted by Boldini. The result, which I hated, was the subject of a brief but animated discussion between us that opened the fissure that was to widen into a roaring river. Boldini showed me seated in a bergère, half turned away from the artist,

but twisting my head around to gaze back at him with an allur-
ing smile of encouragement, as if to reward his artistic efforts.
Much of a long ivory neck and sloping rounded shoulders was
enticingly revealed, and the viewer's eye was led down over a
voluptuously curved torso, clad in black silk and sequins, to an
almost lasciviously jutted rump. It was Boldini at his most lubri-
cious; I might have been the adulterous heroine of a Paul Bour-
get novel greeting her lover in a *maison de passe*. I told Adrian
firmly that I would not hang it in our house.

He laughed, I thought, rather coarsely. "Not if I keep it in my
study?"

"And show it to the gentlemen after dinner? Certainly not.
You can keep it in your dressing room, if you like."

"Aren't you being a bit hard on a great artist, Zelina? After
all, he only paints what he sees."

"Exactly! And when he paints a woman, that's *all* he sees!"

"Is there so much more, really?"

"Just what are you trying to tell me, Adrian?"

"Simply the truth about your famous beauty, my dear. Why
do you suppose it was given you but to lure men?"

"*Lure* men? How do you mean? Like the Lorelei?"

"Precisely."

"Are you implying that I landed you on the rocks?"

"No, but you might have if I hadn't learned to swim."

"I seem to recall a time when you had a nobler concept of
what you choose to term my 'beauty.'"

"That, my loved one, was when you were *most* the Lorelei.
All I heard was the beautiful song."

I decided not to go on with this discussion until I had the time
to consider its implications. Yes, I was like that. I had a considerable control over my temper. Indeed, I think I can boast that I
am that rare woman who knows the exact time in which to
make a scene with her man.

In the next days I did a lot of thinking about my husband and the change in his attitude towards me. Had he chosen Boldini because he knew that this artist would portray me as a vulgar lure, something that a husband could use and *own*, a property and hence a part, and only a humble part, of himself? I was beginning to understand that he was actually jealous of my social success in London. He must have assumed that he was the lord and provider of beautiful things, the author of popular romances, the dashing cosmopolitan figure that made even the oldest societies in Europe consider whether they might not have to reevaluate the brash and opulent republic across the seas. And now it seemed to be his bride, his beautiful bride, rather than himself, who was inducing them to take a second look at America!

I also learned something from the great Henry James, a cousin of Adrian's late mother, whom we had visited on two occasions at his charming red brick town house in Rye. Adrian had professed the greatest admiration of the "master," as he called him, but after our second visit his tone had altered, and he spoke half-contemptuously of the "verbose and lapidary" style of the novelist's later period as blocking out any serious view of the human characters delineated. My new intuition sought the sore spot where Adrian's pride had been wounded, and I thought back on our visits with Mr. James (who incidentally had made much of me) and recalled that his elaborate avoidance of any evaluation of my husband's fiction, despite the latter's constant prodding, must have meant that he had no high regard for it. His sole reference, accompanied by a wicked little wink, was to "the perfervid excitement of dear Adrian's constantly adulterous and so often apprehended heroines."

And indeed Adrian later admitted to me that the master had declined to consider his last novel in a proposed survey of recent American writing!

I had not read Mr. James before, but I did so now, and it opened my eyes to the deficiencies of Adrian's style. My husband had a vivid, if rather fulsome vocabulary, and he could tell a good story, but what he poured into his feverishly written pages was simply the external of the great social world that he found so colorful: the castles and palaces with their glittering interiors, the duels and the balls and the waltzes. It was the method of Disraeli, or, better perhaps, of Scott. But James extracted the essence of the lovely exteriors of the lives of his characters to furnish a glowing backdrop against which to view their stripped souls and to intensify the moral beauty of his dramatic conflicts. I was later to see the Venetian palazzo in *The Wings of the Dove*, that ancient and historic decaying marble edifice gently lapped by the waves of the Grand Canal, as the perfect shell in which to place his dying and exquisite heroine.

But I am straying from our London life. Adrian and I had a brief but revealing exchange one night after a dinner party in which I ventured to suggest that he relaxed his high standards of taste and intellect for the peerage.

"You extol the qualities of wit and imagination," I observed, "but they seem to be less in demand when the lineage is old and the bank balance high."

"Alistair and his spouse belong to history, my dear," he retorted, referring to our hosts of the evening. "They transport me to the court of Charles II. Have you *no* imagination for such things?"

"Not unless they bring me some of the *bons mots* for which that court was famous. You wouldn't go back to Alfred the Great for the plumbing, would you?"

He shrugged as if to give me up. "An ancient peerage to you is just a tag, I suppose. To me it can be a tapestry of great events."

What was the point of going on with *that* discussion? Even

Adrian's much vaunted liberalism in politics now became suspect to me. I guessed that the only thing he really objected to in a system of free enterprise was that he didn't have a larger share of the enterprises.

Our first big crisis in the rising tide of my husband's jealousy came at the great ball given by the duchess of Devonshire to celebrate the queen's diamond anniversary, probably the most famous fancy dress affair since Cleopatra was brought to Caesar in a blanket and the ultimate gala in that age of galas and crowns and glitz. The prince of Wales came as the grand prior of the Order of Saint John in Jerusalem, the princess as Marguerite de Valois, Daisy of Pless as the Queen of Sheba, Lady Randolph Churchill as the Empress Theodora, *et ainsi de suite*. I appeared as the ill-fated Lady Jane Grey, and Adrian, as Philip II — the former husband of her executioner, Bloody Mary! Needless to say, he had fussed for days over our costumes, which were as exact in historical detail as they were rich in texture.

The gentleman whose attentions to myself Adrian chose to resent that night was one who, I admit, might have aroused the jealousy of any husband. It was none other than the famous Harry Cust, almost unrecognizably handsome and dashing as Beau Brummel, who had been the lover of so many peeresses that he came to be known in London society as the father of the House of Lords. He had paid me some pseudogallant attention at other parties — I think he rather fancied our appearance as a striking couple — but he was one of those rare men who can detect the woman whom his charm fails to dazzle, and he had good-naturedly accepted the fact that to me he would be only an amusing fellow guest. Adrian, however, would never have understood this, and I rather enjoyed the sight of him glaring at Harry and me across the ballroom. Indeed, it animated my chatter.

"Do you have parties like this in America, Mrs. Doremus?" Harry was asking.

"Oh, all the time!"

"And on such a scale? As you see, we have plundered our attics, ransacked our museums, bought out our costumers!"

"But who taught you? My countrymen. Or rather my countrywomen. Look at the Americans here tonight. Don't be put off by their titles. We know them as Consuelo Vanderbilt, Minnie Stevens, Mary Leiter, May Goelet, Jennie Jerome. The French say: *cherchez la femme*. They might put it: *cherchez l'or*."

"True, but don't underestimate British greed. We have our own gold here tonight as well. And African gold, Indian gold, an empire's gold!"

"Then it's gold that unites us! That fancy dress party has the same function in New York as in London! The new money loves to dress up in feudal robes and strut about the room like long dead kings and queens. Even your Prince of Wales is what Adrian likes to call a burgher."

"Oh, he perhaps most of all! But your husband himself is no exception to his rule."

I turned to see Adrian approaching us across the floor with a grim countenance. "He looks like his armada," I said with a giggle. "You don't happen to have a storm handy, do you?"

"My wife is tired, Mr. Cust." Adrian's tone was curt. "I think the time has come for me to take her home."

"But, my dear sir, the room thunders with royalty! You can hardly leave before them. And if you will permit me to say so, Mrs. Doremus, if fatigued, has wonderfully concealed it. You would be cruel to deprive the duchess's ball of its brightest adornment."

"I think that I and not you, Mr. Cust, may be the best judge of what is best for Mrs. Doremus."

Harry rose at this and looked Adrian in the eye. If insolence was what the man wanted, his look expressed, the man would certainly have it. "King Philip seems to have brought his high Spanish manners to British soil. May I remind him that Queen Mary Tudor is dead?" He turned to me with a little bow. "*She* would have only cut off your head. I fear he intends to cast you to the flames."

Adrian made a threatening step towards Harry, but I intervened quickly, taking my husband's arm and pulling him away. We left the party, giving our hostess the impression that I had the always acceptable excuse of a young bride, and in the carriage going home I provided Adrian with his first real scene.

"Let me tell you what I shall go as at the next ball we're invited to! *If* we're ever invited to another after Harry tells people how you behaved. I shall ride into the ballroom on a white palfrey, stark naked, as Lady Godiva! And every man in the room will gawk at me and sneer at you for the hammy Othello you are!"

"You had better remember what happened to Desdemona!"

"I don't *care* what happened to Desdemona! It's better to be smothered than live with such an ass as you!"

In the light of a streetlamp I suddenly saw the dangerous bulge of a vein in Adrian's forehead. I decided to be silent and refused to respond to any of his now furious comments. At home I went to a separate bedroom and locked my door. I knew that he kept a pistol in his bureau, and I was having my first doubts as to his sanity. For all my boast I had no wish to share Desdemona's fate.

The next morning Adrian said nothing at all about my scene, or even his, and we continued our life together, with lengthening periods of a rather ominous silence, like two nations which hope that a border incident will not escalate into war. He even offered to have me painted again, this time by an artist of my choice, as I would not allow him to hang the Boldini over the central fireplace in the drawing room. I chose Prince Peter Zoko-rov and made an appointment to go to his studio.

Zokorov was a familiar figure in London society. One of sev-eral minor portraitists who "did" the people who couldn't afford Sargent's fat fee or for whom that master didn't have time, he was a competent artist, but neither a particularly enthusiastic nor a particularly dedicated one. He created likenesses because he had to support himself; he would have much preferred to farm the multitudinous acres of the beloved family estate on the Black Sea. But these had been lost to his father by disinheri-tance; the senior Prince Zokorov had married an actress and been cut off with a ruble. Peter had been raised in France by parents who had been loving and happy even in their reduced circumstances; he had adopted the cheerfulness and optimism of the best kind of Gaul and, alone now at thirty-five, a popular extra man and adequately busy with his oils, he exuded a mild serenity that had no element of the smug.

It did not occur to my husband to be jealous of Peter. Adrian was as unimaginative as a romantic novelist could be. Because Peter was diminutive in stature and plain of feature, he was dis-qualified in Adrian's eye for the category of *jeune premier*. He did not feel the charm of Peter's laughing, large, blue-gray eyes or the infectious quality of his chuckle. When Peter grinned he seemed almost a boy, and a delightful one. I had very much en-joyed his company at London gatherings, and it was more for the prospect of lively chats in his studio than from my admira-tion of his artistry that I chose him to paint me.

I think I must have suspected from the beginning that he was in love with me. But I'm sure I felt at the same time that he would never declare himself to a married woman unless he had reason to believe that she took a relaxed view of her marriage vow. He was no Harry Cust. His eyes seemed only to tell me that there could be no harm in a respectful admiration. Yet London gossip rated him an effective lover, and I had little doubt he was that. I also had little doubt that he was sufficiently aware of the effect on myself of his patent admiration.

We talked at my sittings in the most relaxed way of our ancestral homes, mine in Virginia and his on the Black Sea, to which the uncle who owned it occasionally invited him. I allowed myself to get almost teary about poor Peyton's Grove, shut up now and left to molder.

"But you may yet return to it," he suggested comfortingly. "Perhaps your husband will not wish to live forever abroad. Doesn't there come a time when every man pines for his native land?"

"But for Adrian that would never be in Virginia!" I exclaimed, almost in indignation. "Oh, no, that would be much too dull for him. He must have the bright lights of the wicked city! But let's not talk about Adrian. Let's talk about something pleasant. Tell me more about your lovely place in the Ukraine. Couldn't you ever get it back?"

"No, my uncle loves it as much as I do. And he will leave it one day to his only child, a daughter, who is equally passionate about it."

"Couldn't you marry her?"

"Marriage is not for me, dear lady. I'm far too poor, and Olga must marry money. Indeed, I believe they have someone already picked out for her."

I dropped the subject, but we continued to discuss our childhoods in the sittings. I loved to hear about his parents, and how his mother had insisted on giving up her stage career to match his father's sacrifice of his inheritance, and had joined him in running the small vineyard they had managed to purchase in Burgundy. I told him how I wished that my mother had had some of that same spirit with which to face seeming disaster.

Peter believed that we were each, in our own way, the victims of lost causes, but lost causes, he maintained, might be the source of deeper and more sensitive lives than victories, which tended to be celebrated with a rather vulgar blare. He liked to quote the recently published American poetess, Emily Dickinson, who wrote that success could be best understood by the defeated and that "to comprehend a nectar requires sorest need." Drinking that nectar, he insisted, might bring us to be hung among what Keats called the "cloudy trophies" of melancholy. Yet Peter never seemed really melancholy at all. He made the idea of melancholy attractive.

I began to suspect that he was dallying with my portrait to prolong the sittings, but I had no objection to this. Our talks were beginning to be more frankly personal. One morning he made an indirect reference to my childless condition.

"There's something I don't understand about your pessimism over the future of your Virginia estate. Even if your husband never cares to live there, isn't it perfectly possible that you may have a son or daughter who will?"

I was silent for a minute. "I don't think I will ever have a child."

"You don't want one?"

"It's not that."

And then I felt an irresistible urge to tell him all. It was almost more of a necessity than an urge. I had no parents, no siblings to confide in, and with my London friends I had only party relationships. I suddenly knew that to talk frankly with this infinitely sympathetic man was my only hope.

I rose from my chair, and recognizing my stance as the prologue to some serious announcement Peter at once laid down his brush and faced me.

"My husband evidently does not want an heir. At least not from me. He has discontinued marital relations."

Peter was wonderful! He simply nodded. Then, after a pause, he added: "I'm not sorry to hear it."

I blurted on, hardly aware of what I was saying. "He says I'm not worthy of him! He says I'm always trying to 'lure' men! He calls me odious names!"

"Leave him, dear Zelina, leave him." He had not used my first name before. It had a very pleasant sound.

"Leave him and go where?"

"Back to Peyton's Grove. Where you belong."

"What heaven! Do you really think I could?"

"You could do anything."

"But how could I run the place? A woman alone, with no money?"

"I'll come over and farm it for you. I'm sick of painting portraits, anyway. I've had a feeling all along that this was going to be my last one. And I know about farming, believe me. I've learned at my uncle's."

"What would the neighbors say?" I laughed, and my laugh, I'm afraid, was a bit hysterical.

"Whatever they want to say."

At this point my husband walked in, as always, without knocking on the studio door. But he showed not the slightest awareness that he had interrupted a climactic scene.

"I think it's time you showed me the famous portrait," he stated abruptly to the immediately deferential Peter. "You've taken as long with it as Michelangelo did with the tomb of Julius II!"

"Certainly, Mr. Doremus."

Adrian walked over to view the portrait, and I joined the two of them to view my own likeness. It was strange, but this was my first sight of it. Peter did not like to have his works seen in progress, and each day after our sitting he would put a cover over the canvas. Now, however, I had a full view of it, and I could see at once that it was indeed finished, that it had probably been finished for some days.

It was stupendous. Infinitely superior to anything of his that I had seen. The background was unusual for a portrait of the time; it showed the influence, I suppose, of the recently accepted French impressionist school. For instead of standing alone I was shown entering a room full of people, presumably a grand party, for the walls seemed paneled, and the suggested brackets and tops of chairs seemed gilded, and the shadowy forms of the supposedly chatting couples, who were half turned away from the new arrival, were darkly clad if male and faintly multi-colored if not. Yet all was subdued to the brilliant pink of my gown, the glitter of my diamond necklace and the . . . radiance, for that is how Peter made it look, of my pale, serene countenance. No woman could have looked as beautiful as he had painted me. I was depicted surveying the chamber with an air of mild greeting, of calm acceptance; I was evidently at home there; I was one of the habitual denizens; I had no quarrel with it. But for all that I was somehow detached; the reality of me lived elsewhere. And to my painter that elsewhere was clearly a far better place in which to live; indeed, it was the only place for me to live.

Adrian, for once, seemed to take it in. "The way you've painted her, Zokorov, makes her appear to be looking for someone. Who's she looking for?"

"Someone I don't think she's going to find."

"What do you mean by that?"

"I mean that Mrs. Doremus has the soul of a poet. I doubt that she will find a fellow poet at that party."

"So she's too good for us, is that it?"

"Much too good."

"Too good for me, I suppose is what you're really implying."

"I imply nothing, Mr. Doremus. You infer."

Adrian at this grew frankly surly. "Well, I think she *is* looking for someone at that party. And I'll wager it's Harry Cust."

Peter became very cool at this. "You choose to interpret my painting, Mr. Doremus. As you are quite misguided in your opinion and presumably undereducated in art criticism, let the artist himself offer you some instruction. I had been interested in doing a picture of the new predator known as the American millionaire. But I found he has been so universally cartooned as to be no longer a viable subject. I therefore decided instead to try to conceive a portrait of his victim or natural prey, and you see before you the result. I have placed her in her native habitat. But in her eyes, the windows of her soul, I have placed hope. And the hope is not only for herself. It is for all of us. On her we must depend."

The blue vein on Adrian's brow whose swelling I had observed on the night of the duchess of Devonshire's ball was once again dangerously enlarged. He glanced furiously from me to Peter to the portrait.

"I'll show you the extent of my dependence!" he shouted and rushed at the picture, snatching from his pocket, to my horror, a penknife. I was moving to restrain him when I felt myself firmly grasped by Peter.

"Let him do what he wants to the picture, Zelina. He commissioned it; it is his."

Adrian gave us a look of hate; then he turned to the picture and proceeded to stab his knife into my painted face until it was just a hole in the canvas. Peter then spoke.

"And now, sir, will you leave this studio, or shall I call the police and show them your act of vandalism?"

"I'm taking my wife with me!"

"Oh, but you're not. She would hardly be safe with such a monster. Or do you wish to argue that with the police as well?"

Adrian uttered some inaudible curse and rushed out of the studio.

I did not follow him, then or later.

❀

Peter and I did go to Peyton's Grove, and he did become a farmer. He painted no more portraits, but he did the charming watercolors that hang all over our walls. The neighbors, curiously enough, seemed to have little to say about our unusual domestic arrangement during the period when Adrian was confined to an asylum, but when he came out, and when he ultimately divorced me, and Peter and I could marry, they all came to call, and we were accepted again as my family always had been. We have been blessed, though no children came, and in time I lost Peter to the little family mausoleum behind what used to be the rose garden.

We were always hard up, and I once suggested that he might consider returning to his portraits.

"No," he said firmly, "I wasn't really any good. I waited for one model, and after I had done her, I realized that my art had been fulfilled. Its real function was to bring her back where she belonged, and that it has done."

My young law school friend tells me that when he has succeeded in his profession and "made his pile," he will buy Peyton's Grove and restore it to its ancient glory. I pray that he may survive the coming war and find himself in a position to do so. But if he doesn't someone else may. Rich Yankees have already bought so many of our old places that one unreconstructed friend of mine had had a fresco painted in her dining room showing all the lovely houses that she used to visit, but where her anti-northern bias now keeps her from calling. I am not like that, but in any event my calling days are over.

I wait now, in total acceptance, for the redbird to come. Of course, I know that he won't come here — although there are two cardinals that live in my garden — but that it will be his mission to visit some Peyton cousin, perhaps as far from Virginia as our embassy in Rome, to convey the news that a family member has gone. And I rather hope that it will not be long.

The Veterans

1.

I HAVE ALWAYS BEEN AWARE of the reason for my almost lifelong interest in Gilbert Everett. Perhaps it would be more accurate to call it a kind of morbid fascination. I seemed to make out in him a silly caricature of myself, a warning of what I, Lyman Evans, might actually turn into if I didn't watch out. It was not that there was any physical resemblance. It was more that I suspected — and quite irrationally feared — some inner compatability of souls.

Gilbert himself was not an interesting man. At Harvard, where we were both members of the class of 1852, he was stoutish and fair, with a round bland countenance and mildly appealing blue eyes; he was earnest and full, too full, of goodwill, and anxious, too anxious, to have everyone else's. It was impossible to dislike him, but though we were cousins — second cousins — he was never, at least at college, one of my intimates. Perhaps I kept him at a certain distance because of the fancied inward resemblance. Might we not both be throwbacks to the great-grandfather we shared? Gilbert, at any rate, had no such compunctions. He cheerfully professed to be my good friend and insisted that our cousinship delightfully confirmed this.

We became closer, inevitably, in that fateful year for our nation, 1860, when we both, for however different reasons, found ourselves domiciled in Paris. We were twenty-eight, and still bachelors. I had joined the foreign service and been appointed second secretary to our minister to the court of Louis-Napoléon. Gilbert had no job or position; possessed of ample means, he was writing a novel (which he never finished) and sharing an apartment on the Rue de Rivoli with the widowed mother whose only child he was.

Mrs. Everett — "Cousin Louisa" to me — had come to France on her husband's death (the deceased had never cared to travel) to find out if the people were as civilized as she had heard, and although she found them both trivial and immoral, she thoroughly approved of their cooking, their sense of order and their architecture, and had decided to remain. She was a small, neat, pale, withered (she had married late) figure, with a tall auburn multi-layered wig and calmly critical gray eyes. She was rigid in her views and in her habits and frequented mostly the small American expatriate community, but as she had a good chef and a handsome flat and spoke the language surprisingly well, she included a small number of moderately important Parisian figures at her receptions.

Cousin Louisa made no bones about her disgust with the seething political cauldron that our capital across the Atlantic had become. Having learned of my anti-slavery convictions, she would lecture me when I called on the horrors of abolitionism.

"Of course in New York we got rid of the 'peculiar' institution long ago, and that's probably as it should be. After all, it has no place with us, for we have no Negroes, or none to speak of. But what earthly business is it of ours if Southerners hang on to it? They've brought these poor creatures over from Africa, and what else are they to do with them? Anyway, it's their problem, not ours. We have enough of our own to solve without borrowing trouble and tearing the country apart. What about the Irish in New York?"

Gilbert was considerably more idealistic than his mother and did not hesitate to argue the cause of emancipation at her table. Cousin Louisa rather enjoyed the liveliness that a difference of opinion added to her little parties, particularly as our remoteness from the American scene kept her guests from waxing too excited, but the nomination of Lincoln made us all graver. Now she would hold up her hand at table to outlaw the subject and emphasize her family ties and connections with the planters of the Old South. Peace had to be kept, and her darling son's pale, white skin not endangered! She even encouraged Gilbert's visits to the house of an American representative of Georgian cotton growers, one Ellsworth Groves, whose daughters she had once deemed too flamboyantly pretty and bold for her modest and gentlemanly boy. She now hoped that their influence might douse some of his excessive liberalism.

The Groveses gave garden parties on the grounds of their charming little château in Neuilly, and the three beautiful and lively daughters attracted male callers from even the most stalwart Yankee families of the American community. Even I allowed myself to be dragged there by Gilbert, and I am forced to admit that our host was so charming, so well informed and so deferential to opposing opinion, that he almost persuaded me that the differences between North and South might be settled by a group of gentlemen over a bottle of port. Yet I was always aware, even back then, that there was an element of steel behind his gracious front. And this was even truer of his two large, easygoing, smiling and elegantly garbed sons.

One afternoon, after our host had politely broken off a discussion with me about the coming presidential election in the States to greet an arriving French senator, I joined Gilbert, who was sitting in an arbor having what appeared to be a spirited argument with one of the Misses Groves. She was taking him to task with mock indignation.

"But I declare, sir, I can't for the life of me see why you Yankee gentlemen have to go stickin' your long noses — in your case, Mr. Everett, a very nice one, if you'll allow a personal remark — into our Southern affairs. What's it to you what people we use to pick our cotton or staff our mansions? You all must jes learn to leave us be. Do we tell you not to employ poor white children fourteen hours a day in your textile factories? It may be a cryin' shame we don't, but we don't."

I reflected that Miss Groves, like even the dizziest Southern belles in this new era, had been doing her homework. But Gilbert was only too happy to take her on. He was waxing oratorical, as he sometimes did now, particularly in female company. He had learned to contradict his mother, and this, he must have felt, had proved his knighthood.

"But I wish you *would* protest the conditions in our factories!" he exclaimed. "I'm sure they're shocking, and we need all the help we can get to remedy the situation. That's the great thing in being one nation. Strong and indivisible. So we can fix everything everywhere. But I have to make one point, Miss Groves, if you will permit me, about our factory workers. I doubt that even the most ill-used and overworked of them would change places with the most pampered slave in the South."

"That, sir, is 'cause they're white. No white man would ever change places with a Nigra."

"I meant he wouldn't change places with a slave. Of any color."

"But there aren't any white slaves. That term means somethin' quite different." Here she giggled, as if at her own boldness.

"Somethin' we ladies aren't meant to know about. No, Mr. Everett, you must teach your friends to leave us alone in our benighted country. Or else one fine day you may wake up to discover we've jes picked up and gone our own way."

"You mean seceded?"

"If that's the word for it."

"But, my dear Miss Groves, that would be treason!"

I had noticed, though Gilbert had not, that one of Miss Groves's brothers had moved closer to our little group and was lending a seemingly casual ear to our discussion. He was a big man, with black curly hair, a square, white, impassive face and small glinting eyes with yellow spots that could reflect anger or friendliness without the least alteration of his features. At the word "treason" I saw the change in them. Yet when he spoke, it was in a pleasant drawl.

"That's a mighty strong word you're using, Mr. Everett. Sometimes at parties on warm summer afternoons with pretty girls and good drinks we use stronger terms than we actually intend. That I'm sure was the case with you just now. Isn't that so?"

Gilbert was evidently much taken aback. "Sorry, sir, I didn't see you. But I'm happy to have you join our little discussion. I was using the word, of course, in a purely technical sense. The withdrawal of a state from the union without the consent of the others or without a constitutional amendment would be an act of rebellion. And surely rebellion is treason, is it not? As a matter of law?"

"Well, that's not quite how some of us see it, sir. Particularly some of us from the sovereign state of Georgia. We hold the union to be a partnership freely entered into and from which any partner may freely withdraw."

"I see that, of course, as an argument. It's a perfectly tenable theory. Most of us Northerners happen to adhere to a more binding concept of the contract. I suppose you and I may agree to disagree."

"Not quite, sir, I'm afraid, not quite." Groves's voice softened as his words grew more ominous. "I find that to my ears, perhaps over-sensitive, the word you used to my sister has an unpleasant ring. Treason. No, I do not like the term. It conjures up a picture of Benedict Arnold. I fear I cannot accept the use of such a word in respect to a legal step that might conceivably one day be taken by my state. Perhaps, sir, under the circumstances, and considering my sensitivity, you will have the goodness to withdraw it."

Gilbert was very pale now. But when he nodded it was almost eagerly. "Certainly, sir. I'll be glad to withdraw it."

But Groves was ineluctable. "But not to me, sir. The word was used to my sister. Will you be good enough as to tell *her* that it is withdrawn?"

Gilbert rose and made an exaggerated bow to Miss Groves. "Please allow me, ma'am, to withdraw the offensive term."

I could see that he was trying to cover up the abjectness of his surrender in a gesture of mock gallantry. But it fooled no one.

When he and I had dinner afterwards on the terrace of a restaurant in the Champs-Élysées, Gilbert, morose and preoccupied, had swallowed half a bottle of burgundy before he allowed himself to broach the subject that was obviously on his mind.

"Of course, you feel that I cringed before the fire-eater!" His eyes were wide with misery.

"Was he a fire-eater? His tone was mild enough."

"Do you know that he killed a man in a duel in Atlanta last year? And that he's supposed to be one of the deadliest shots even in that formidable town!"

I shrugged. "Let us be thankful then that your little episode ended peacefully."

"But you're still sneering at me. Even if you don't show it.

You think I was lily-livered. You think I should have stuck to my guns and then let that hothead call me out and slaughter me in cold blood!"

"Gilbert, you're being ridiculous. I think you behaved just as you should have. And the last thing that we want, with things as tense as they are at home, is a duel before the eyes of all Paris over the issue of secession."

"Particularly with the representative of the North ending up with a bullet through his head!"

"You handled the situation the only way you could. But in the future I suggest you use more temperate language in discussing our national differences when Southerners are present. Particularly Southern gentlemen."

"Oh, you think I was showing off to the lady? And backed right down when I saw her brother?"

Well, that *was* what happened, wasn't it? Yet I tried to soothe him. "If you had provoked a duel, Gilbert, you would have been as irresponsible as your opponent."

"Well, all I can say is that I hope he and his ilk get their come-uppance if they provoke a war! I hope and pray that they'll get their fill of bullets and gunpowder! Think what a terrible thing a duel is, Lyman! To have to stand there on the terrain while your bloodthirsty opponent coolly raises his pistol and aims it directly at your head or heart! To know that in another second he may blot you out, with all your youth and health and high hopes of a wonderful and exciting life! Oh, just imagine it! That one minute you have the whole world at your feet, and the next it's blown to bits because of a silly word taken the wrong way by a hothead at a party you probably didn't want to go to in the first place."

"But a man doesn't have to duel," I pointed out. "We've pretty well knocked it out at home, at least in the North."

"But not in the South," Gilbert went on gloomily. "And not in France, where we are. And certainly not in most European countries. It's so unfair. Like war. Why should one generation be slaughtered and mutilated and another live happily in peace? Why, if war comes at home, should untold numbers of young men 'go to their graves like beds,' as Hamlet says, while their sons and grandsons may live and make money? Is it fair?"

"Since when was life fair?"

Everything Gilbert said about the duel was undeniable; I had no quarrel with that. But he should have refused the retraction and then declined the duel. He might have looked yellow to the French (unless they attributed his attitude to some American eccentricity), and he would have certainly been shamed in the eyes of our Southern compatriots, but should he have really minded that? What stuck in my craw was that he had been brave in the presence of a woman and humble in that of a man.

The election of Lincoln was followed by the secession of the Southern states and, early in 1861, by the president's call for volunteers to suppress the rebellion. Gilbert and his mother were wintering in Cannes at the time, but he was even further from my thoughts, which were totally engaged in the conflict between my duties at the office and my felt duty to go home and enlist. This was resolved at last by Mr. John Bigelow, who had arrived to serve as American consul in Paris and who gave me a straight talk, which left me no alternative.

He was a fine, vigorous figure of a gentleman, handsome, a bit formidable, cultivated, polite and down-to-earth in his assessment of the international situation. It was no secret in the diplomatic corps that he enjoyed the confidence of Secretary of State Seward and that it was into his hands, even more than into those of the minister, that the vital job of keeping Napoléon III and his government neutral had been entrusted.

"I know of course that you want to fight, my dear Lyman." He addressed me so as an old New York friend of my late father's. "Any young man of spirit like yourself must be itching to get into the fray and bring these crazy rebels to their senses. But you've got a tougher job, which is to stay right here and help me to keep Bonaparte from sticking his imperial snout into our business. This war is going to be longer and harder than most people think, and it will be even longer and harder if Britain and France should ever recognize the Confederacy. You may ask me why I need a young man like you for the job here and why I can't get someone older. The answer is that you know the ropes and the language and the court at the Tuileries. And that there's nobody else over here available and no time to train them if there were. Minister Adams in London is hanging on to his son Henry, who's raring to go home and fight, and I'm going to do the same with you. You're in the front lines here, my boy, as much as if you were toting a musket in Virginia. And your father would have agreed with me if he was alive, believe me."

I have to admit that Mr. Bigelow's proposition did not come to me entirely as a disappointment. From boyhood I had suffered from the apprehension that military combat might find me something less than a hero. It was, of course, my glorious military father who, certainly unintentionally, had instilled this concern in me. Ever since he had returned from the Mexican War, full of gory stories about that brief but successful struggle, I had nursed the gloomy conviction that Mars visited our earth periodically to teach each generation of males what it was to be a *man*. There had been, of course, our splendid revolution, and then the War of 1812, then Mexico, and there would be in time, inevitably, a further bloodletting for the benefit of my age group. When I mentioned my theory to Father, he did not find it a grim one; he had obviously relished his little war; it had been short and picturesque and triumphant, and with few casualties, at least on our side. He had been a West Point graduate who had left the army to make money on Wall Street and been only too happy to leave the perhaps faintly boring domestic bliss that my poor mother provided to head up a regiment at the behest of President Polk. His had always been a fine, strong, cheerful, booming military presence, which had filled his only son, however much petted and coddled, with the apprehension that the paternal valor could never be equalled and that any filial effort to do so would invite invidious comparisons.

Now why could I not have instead fantasized myself on a great stallion charging up the slopes of Chapultepec? To begin with, I never enjoyed my father's stature; I was adequately but much more modestly built, and I had never excelled as an athlete. Also, I inherited my mother's more passive nature and her love of books and music. I even shared her intense sympathy with pain and suffering, not only in fellow humans but with birds and animals. And I certainly saw war as the event most likely to create human agony at its cruellest. There was one story that Father particularly liked to tell — after dinner over the port when the ladies had retired to the parlor — and that I particularly dreaded. It regarded the terrible suffering of one of his sergeants who had to undergo a leg amputation in a crude hospital tent without anesthetic other than a bottle of whiskey on a field at the outskirts of Mexico City. The poor man's only uttered complaint was that it hadn't been rum!

Did I then enter the foreign service with an idea of evading my destiny? Did I hope against hope that if I were safely abroad when war broke out that it would be too late or too difficult for me to return to join the fray? One thing at least is certain. I had — and *before* my interview with Mr. Bigelow — requested official permission to resign my post and enlist. And I had so written to my widowed mother, who had replied with her usual simplicity and acceptance: "It is what your father would have expected; I must be brave and silent." I had actually been enjoying something like exhilaration at the thought of myself in uniform. It had been good at last to have the awful threat of shame evaporated. Now I could only fight. Now I could only die. Now I should have peace.

But Mr. Bigelow had changed all that. There could be no question of my opposing his plans for me; it would have been akin to deserting my battalion in the heat of battle. Whatever Mr. Lincoln's representative defined as my post was where I had to stay. And if the war turned out to be as long as Mr. Bigelow supposed, there would surely be ample time for him to find an ultimate replacement for one of my duties. In the meantime my work was cut out, and I threw myself into it with a kind of fury. But the worst part was that, dependent on slow mails as we were, there were frustrating days in which there was little or nothing to do at the office, and I would frantically dream up excuses to call on bored imperial officials in vain efforts to stimulate enthusiasm for the Union cause, and accept the dullest invitations to dinner on the chance that I might find the opportunity to present it to Southern sympathizers.

When Gilbert returned to Paris from the Riviera in the spring — his mother, he said, had refused to come back earlier — he showed up at my office to talk anxiously about what he could do to help in the war effort.

"I suppose you could always go home and sign up."

"And leave Mother? All to herself over here? There's no conscription, is there?"

"Not yet."

"It may sound conceited, but it seems to me there are a lot of things I could do better than be a soldier. What you do, for example." He glanced about my office, as if to imply that any decently educated man should be able to shuffle those papers. His attitude was innocuous enough, but it riled me. When he went on, he didn't make things any better. "And I shouldn't need any salary. I'd be happy to work for nothing."

"Which is what you'd be worth, at least till I'd trained you." But I saw now that his eyes were pleading. He *did* want to do something, and I relented. "I'll speak to Mr. Bigelow."

Mr. Bigelow listened with a mild sympathy when I mentioned Gilbert's availability. His wife, it turned out, had been acquainted with Cousin Louisa in New York.

"I suppose your friend has some health problem that would keep him out of military service. I don't, of course, wish to deprive the army of a good soldier."

"He's not actually physically unfit, sir, but I doubt he has the temperament of a fighting man. I venture to suggest he'd be more use to us here than to General McClellan."

"Hmm." Mr. Bigelow did not see this as much of an endorsement. "My wife called on his mother the other day. She found a cozy little expatriate group there. They were nothing if not tepid, she said, on the subject of the war."

"Gilbert doesn't share his mother's views, sir, or those of her friends. I have always found him sound on slavery and secession."

But Mr. Bigelow was now taken up by his strong views on Americans abroad. He even banged his desk. "Still, he lives in that little nest of near treason. Those people think America isn't good enough for them, and they run after European titles. They think the only aristocracy we have left on our side of the Atlantic is in the Old South. They sneer at Mr. Lincoln as a rail-splitter and maintain that Jeff Davis, at least, is a gentleman. Oh, I have an eye on them! And you can be damn sure

I'm not going to let them squeeze a little rat into my office to alert them to any Union setbacks we may have the bad luck to encounter!"

I was a bit ashamed of my inner glow of satisfaction that this small carpet of evasion should be so summarily ripped from under poor Gilbert's trembling feet. But as I rose to leave, another carpet was pulled from under my own.

"Wait a minute, Lyman. I shouldn't let myself get so impatient. You tell me your friend won't require a salary, so we wouldn't have to get State Department approval. Very well, if you really believe he'd be no use to the army and might be of some to you here, and if you'll guarantee that he won't leak any secrets to unfriendly ears, take him on, by all means. He might even be a bit of a spy for you, in his mother's salon! All I ask is that you assure me he isn't simply looking for an excuse to avoid the conscription bill that is surely coming."

I hesitated, but only for a moment. Then I heard myself say, very clearly: "No, sir, I'm afraid I can't give you my word about that."

"Well, there you are, my boy, there you are! There's got to be a limit to what you do for old college chums. Tell Mr. Everett to lose himself, and in the fastest way possible!"

I was not very happy with myself in the next few days. Gilbert took his rejection quietly enough, but I could see that he was bitterly disappointed, and I blushed when he thanked me warmly for my intercession. But was I expected to tell a lie to a man like Bigelow to protect a friend? And of course Gilbert was trying to avoid the draft! Could anyone doubt that?

Well, needless to say I saw less of Gilbert after this. But he also seemed less anxious to see me. He probably didn't want to have to explain his continued failure to go home to join the colors. But when the first conscription bill was passed, I wondered, out of simple curiosity, what effect it would have on him.

This I was to learn, some weeks after the enactment, when I finally made a Saturday afternoon call on Cousin Louisa. I had, of course, been avoiding her little parties since Bigelow's denunciation of them, but I didn't want to drop a relative altogether. I found Gilbert alone in the parlor. He said his mother would be in shortly and that he was glad to have this chance to chat.

"I suppose you know all about this draft law? Does it apply to residents abroad?"

I made little effort to conceal my small relish for the direction of his curiosity. "I don't think that's entirely clear. Certainly they are not specifically exempted. But I doubt you have to worry, Gilbert. Mr. Lincoln has enough on his hands without scouring the capitals of Europe in search of draft dodgers. And if he did, I doubt that Louis-Napoléon, who is praying for a rebel victory to give him a free hand in Mexico, would cooperate in extraditing them."

Gilbert drew himself up at this with considerable dignity. "That's not my concern at all, Lyman. I asked the question only in the hope that *should* I go home to enlist, it would not be deemed simply that I *had* to."

"Does it really matter, if you're going to go, anyway, whether it's to obey your conscience or the law?"

Gilbert took a step closer to me and stared earnestly up in my face. "Tell me frankly. In my position would *you* go?"

"How can you ask me to tell *you* what to do?" I exclaimed in exasperation. "Can't you see that my own exemption makes it impossible?"

He nodded. "Of course, I have Mother to consider. But I've told her that if the draft covers me, I must go. She can't really object to that. The law's the law. She always made a great point of that. She even used to argue that Northerners should obey the Fugitive Slave Act."

"And I still do!" Cousin Louisa had appeared in the doorway

and had taken in her son's last remarks. "I am all for obeying the law. But this law no longer covers you, my son."

"Is that what your lawyer tells you? Is that what you went to see him about when the bill was passed? That it has no extra-territorial effect? Why didn't you tell me?"

"Because, my dear, I've only just found out." She held up a letter. "My lawyer told me the bill offered any draftee exemption for three hundred dollars, and he sent in my check that very day. And here's my answer! You are a free man, my boy!"

"I can still go," he muttered.

"And waste your mother's three hundred bucks!" I'm afraid it was I who was guilty of this bit of bad taste. "I thought you were so proud of your Scottish heritage!"

"You can still do anything you want," Cousin Louisa responded with greater dignity. "The point is that you can now make up your own mind about time and place and degree of commitment. You can exercise your own good judgment as to whether your poor back that has been giving you so much trouble of late is strong enough to carry you on long wet marches through Virginia. You needn't be at the mercy of some army sawbones who is probably under orders to certify every draftee as good cannon fodder."

Gilbert was rather sullenly silent, and when I took my early leave of them it was with an invitation that they come to my flat the following Monday to hear a lecture with photographs by the *Éclair* newspaperman René Bouffon, who was just back from a trip to cover the fighting in Virginia. Cousin Louisa declined, and Gilbert, without committing himself, accompanied me down to the street, where he suggested a turn in the Tuileries Gardens. For some minutes we strolled in silence in the mild spring weather amid the nursemaids and dogs and the shrilly playing, charmingly dressed French children.

"You despise me," he said at last, in a level tone.

"My dear fellow, what are you talking about?"

"You know perfectly well. You despise me because you think I'm going to allow my mother to get me out of the draft."

"Gilbert, she's already done so! Who am I to set myself up to judge you?"

"I don't know who you are to do that, but I know you've done it. You think I'm hiding behind Mother's apron strings. You think I'm too yellow to go home and fight!"

"I can't imagine your mother in an apron. And, anyway, all sorts of men at home are buying exemption from conscription. We get reports of that in the office. It's become a perfectly respectable thing to do."

"*If* you have a proper excuse. Like a wife and children to support. Or some work, like yours, that's more important than shooting bullets at rebs. But I haven't got anything like that."

"You've got your mother."

"You think she really needs me that much?"

I had to be silent.

"You see? But there's one thing I've decided I don't have to endure. And that's your contempt."

"Gilbert, I promise you —"

"Please, Lyman. I *know* how you feel. There's no point in your denying it. And I've made up my mind. I'm going home to join up. It may kill Mother, but on the other hand it may not. There's a side of every mother that doesn't too much mind seeing her boy in uniform."

"Except she won't see you in it."

"She may. She might even come home with me. I'm counting on you to arrange passage. It's probably better to go on a French vessel, isn't it? To avoid Confederate raiders?"

"Gilbert, will you listen to me?"

"No, I won't, Lyman. In fact, I'm going back to the apartment. I'll come to see you in your office tomorrow, if I may, to discuss our travel plans."

I slumped in dismay to a bench and watched that somehow now sturdier little figure march back to the street. And then I suddenly pictured him lying horribly prone and dead on the red dirt of a Virginia field, his lips agape, his eyes blankly looking upward, a huge red hole on his brow and head. For I had seen Bouffon's terrible photographs. "Shooting bullets at rebs," poor Gilbert had said! As if he could ever have hit one! And it was I who would have sent this harmless and unharming lamb to the slaughterhouse, and why? Because I had the temerity to judge him a poltroon! Cousin Louisa would be able to accuse me of killing her son as surely as if I had pressed the trigger.

I jumped up now to hurry after my friend. I found him in the office of his concierge, looking over some just delivered mail.

"Gilbert," I urged him. "Please come to Monsieur Bouffon's lecture on Monday. I know your mother won't, but I particularly want you to, anyway."

"I'm sorry, Lyman, but under the circumstances I think I should spend as many of my evenings with Mother as possible."

"Please spare me just this one. I really need your help. And remember. You're going to owe me one if I work out your passage."

"Oh, well, if you put it that way."

My audience on Monday night was carefully selected from those of the American community whose sympathies were more formal than fervent for the Union cause, and a smattering of French society folk to whom the conflict across the seas seemed largely the opportunity to weaken a potentially formidable opponent to Gallic imperial interests. But they listened with interest to Bouffon's lurid account of the aftermath of the Battle of

Antietam. He had visited the terrain before the dead had been buried and while the wounded were still being retrieved, and he had lost much of his concern for his emperor's point of view in his unfeigned horror of what he had witnessed.

"It's war on a scale we've never visualized over here," he related to the silent group. "Unless perhaps in the retreat from Moscow in 1813. And *that* broke Napoléon. The camp hospitals can't begin to cope with the wounded on both sides. It's a terrible thing to see a great nation tearing itself to shreds before one's eyes. You all know the old saying that there's no savagery like that of a civil war. Our own religious conflicts of the sixteenth century are proof of that. How any man who's out of it would want to get in, or any man in it not want to get out, is beyond me. This war should be stopped at all costs. In the simple name of humanity!"

Gilbert did not talk to me after the lecture about his reactions to the reporter's account; in fact I noted that he avoided me. He had clearly been too upset to wish to discuss it; his features were almost green. The photographs had indeed been ghastly, too much so, as one old French nobleman had indignantly pointed out to me afterwards, for a gathering that included ladies. Two such had actually left in the middle of the showing. I had let my enthusiasm for our cause a bit run away with me.

Gilbert did not come to my office the next day as planned, nor indeed in the following weeks. His back, he wrote me, was "acting up badly," and the departure for America would have to be postponed. The postponements were repeated, and I soon accepted the evident fact that Gilbert deemed himself too ill even to think of enlisting.

He now, it appeared, had to spend part of every week stretched out on a chaise longue, unable to stand up long enough before a mirror to shave. But he had started to keep a map of the positions of the Union and rebel armies, and one of the uses to him of my occasional visits was to obtain the latest information on military movements. He seemed to think that he might be making a contribution to the cause by keeping abreast of the war news, that he might somehow accelerate the end of a national agony that was becoming too much his own. When would it be over? he kept beseeching me. Would it *ever* be over?

Well, it was certainly looking better. The tide of battle had turned in 1863 when the great double victories of Vicksburg and Gettyburg resounded through the chancellories of Europe, crushing into pulp the gloomy predictions of imperialist statesmen and proclaiming the emergence of a vast new power that would forever bar colonization to the west. Oh, how I loved that time! My heart throbbed with joy at social gatherings where I now found myself warmly greeted by potentates who had formerly offered me only the tips of their fingers. I never had even silently to let my lips form the words "I told you so"; the facts shouted them in every ear.

Some years later, in Washington, I compared my Parisian memories of the last two years of the war with those of Henry Adams, who had spent them as his father's secretary in London. He had experienced the same exultation. "As the first great military blows began to fall," he told me, "I curled up in bed in the silence of night to listen with incredulous hope." Like me, he had felt the shivers of Europe as a great new power emerged across the ocean that would change the fate of the world.

By Appomattox Gilbert's back had rendered him a partial invalid, and if I was to see him at all I had to call at Cousin Louisa's, where he spent much of his day reclining on a couch in a silk robe smoking cigarettes when he was not working on his maps. It did not surprise me that his ailment was not immediately cured with the cessation of hostilities. Too sudden a convalescence might have caused tongues to wag — at least my tongue. When I bid goodbye to him, for I had been ordered home for a tour of duty in the State Department, he waved a wan hand sadly at the war maps he had so assiduously kept, as if Othello's occupation were now gone. No one, he seemed to be telling me, could say that *he* had not done his bit.

2.

I did not see Gilbert for six years, but we exchanged letters, and I learned that he was slowly recovering his health, that, indeed, he was at last resuming a normal life. The war with Prussia, however, and the siege of Paris and particularly the horrors of the Commune, convinced him and his mother that France was no longer the capital of civilization, and they returned to their native land to reopen the Everett brownstone on lower Park Avenue and the ornate Italianate Everett villa on Bellevue Avenue in Newport. As I had frequently to revisit my native New York from Washington to keep a watchful eye on our family real estate after my father's death, I had occasion to call again on my cousins. I found that Gilbert had established a kind of salon in the gilded and curlicued Louis Philippe parlor of the family mansion, mixing old Knickerbocker New York with writers and painters of academic respectability. It was moderately amusing, at least by the standards of the eighteen seventies.

Cousin Louisa, who was showing her years now (she had been over forty when Gilbert was born), was much featured by her son, who was always fussing about her and showing her off, but it was quite evident to me, and certainly to her, that she had been superseded as the dominant member of the household.

"He treats me as if I were some sort of *monument historique*," she complained to me one afternoon. " 'Do you know that Mother even knew Lafayette?' he asks people. He claims he's putting together a salon like Madame Récamier. And he actually imitates her in using only two words to people when they arrive and leave: *Enfin!* to the first and *Déjà?* to the second. Humpf! He'd better not get them mixed up! Oh, you'll find we're very Bohemian now, Lyman. Scribblers and daubers mix with the *crème de la crème*. And don't ever even in joke, I beg you" — here Cousin Louisa raised her hands in mock horror — "refer to me, as you once did, as your favorite copperhead. Oh, we're all for the Stars and Stripes! And we always were, too, right through the war! Don't forget that. You thought, my dear cousin, that *you* stayed in Paris to keep Napoléon the Little, as we call him now, neutral. But where would you have been without the help of the Everetts, mother and son — oh, yes, even *me*, Lyman, according to Gilbert — fighting the lonely battle against French pro-Southern prejudice?"

Cousin Louisa, I made out, was too maternal to wish to spoil her only child's playing any social game he wanted, but she was not above the temptation to share the irony of it with at least one old friend and relative.

I began to feel, on my visits to Cousin Louisa and Gilbert, that the former was being a bit eased into the background, very unlike what their relative positions had been in Paris. It was not in any way that Gilbert slighted his mother; indeed, he rather talked her up, but she was distinctly aging, and the bright little group that assembled around his armchair to exchange quips in what he must have imagined to have been the fashion of the eighteenth-century salon of a Madame du Deffand or a Mademoiselle de Lespinasse, tended to leave the old girl more or less to herself in a corner. It was there that I chose to join her, partly for good family manners but more for my growing aversion to the affectation of Gallic deportment exhibited by Gilbert's younger visitors.

It was during one of these visits that I had a sudden glimpse of a very different woman in my elderly cousin than the one I had thought I knew. I had asked Cousin Louisa if she wouldn't prefer to join a group.

"No, Lyman, I'm quite content with my little corner. But you go. Don't feel you have to entertain an old body like me. You've done your duty. Now, scat!"

"But, Cousin Louisa, I regard you as the light of the party!"

"Go on. I know what you really think of me. I knew it in Paris. You said yourself I was your favorite copperhead. But I guess those old issues are behind us now. Or should be."

"They don't seem to be with Gilbert."

"No, they don't, do they? And do you know something? I think he's beginning to be actually ashamed of me."

"Ashamed of you! How?"

"Because I wasn't a firebrand for the Union during the war. As if it mattered what an old lady living abroad was or wasn't! But he seems to have got it into his head that my attitude gave him a bad name at the time and that it may still be doing him harm."

"How could it?"

"Well, you see, he now takes the position that he was a passionate patriot all during the war and was kept out of the army only because of his health. He's even built this into a major personal tragedy. And he's talking about writing a book about the Reconstruction of the South. Oh, he's very severe on the subject of our poor defeated Southern brothers! I'm afraid he thinks even the carpetbaggers are too good for them."

"Well, Southerners *did* start the war, you know."

"I know, I know." She nodded. "But haven't they suffered enough?"

"Tell me, Cousin Louisa, when did you develop this great sympathy for lost causes? Was it after Sedan, and the flight of Napoléon and his lovely Eugénie? I remember how you admired her."

"I admired her *looks*. Who didn't? I never admired the shoddy Second Empire. All glitter and little substance. But you'll be surprised, I think, Lyman, by my answer to your question. I learned my sympathy for losers after the fall of the Commune in 1871."

At this she had my full attention. "*You*, Cousin Louisa! A sympathizer with communists? With the mob that murdered the archbishop of Paris? Wasn't he even a friend of yours?"

"He was, poor man. But you see, Lyman, I saw what happened to that mob. You remember my apartment was on the Rue de Rivoli. I witnessed with my own eyes the burning of the Tuileries. And I was horrified. I had no sympathy then for those crazy anarchists. I wouldn't have cared if they'd all been shot. But then they all *were*! I saw soldiers brutally hustle a crowd of young men — *and* women — down the street under my balcony and into a yard where they were slaughtered, every last one of them! Something turned over inside of me, and it hasn't turned back since."

"I don't wonder. And where was Gilbert when all this was going on?"

"He was safe in a sanatorium in Switzerland where he had gone for a cure. I was glad at the time that he had been spared what I saw, but now I sometimes wonder if it wouldn't have done him good."

"I think I see what you mean."

"It might have kept him from tooting the trumpet of victory quite so loudly. It doesn't become a man who hasn't been engaged in the actual fighting. You would never be guilty of that, Lyman. You're too much of a gentleman."

Ah, how her words stung me! Yet she never meant them to. She had no conception of my tortured misgivings at what I privately called my "paper war" as opposed to a shooting one. Her practical woman's mind drew no particular distinction between

Gilbert's and my failure to bear arms. The only important point was that we had *not* borne them — it didn't so much matter why — and, not having borne them, we shouldn't boast about the victory. A man's inner turmoil as to whether his excuse was adequate, as to whether he was brave or yellow in availing himself of it, was of little interest and less importance to her. She made me feel that her sex, with all its disadvantages, might have been the better one into which to have been born.

"You've certainly given me a lot to think about," I told her gravely as I rose to take my leave. "Maybe every morning, before I go to the office, I should devote a few minutes to a silent reverie of what it must be like to be a reconstructed Southerner."

"Do so, my friend. It won't do you a bit of harm. And then tell Gilbert what effect it has on you. But I greatly fear he will not heed you."

It was fortunate indeed that I had the talk when I did, for Cousin Louisa lived only a week after it. She had had, unbeknownst to me, a couple of small strokes, and a third one carried her off, blessedly, when she was sleeping.

3.

Gilbert now gave all his energies to his salon. He rarely went out; if you wanted the right people to call on you, he told me, you had better be home when they called. He could always be found, at half after four in the afternoon, and for two hours thereafter, stretched out on a chaise longue if it happened to be a day when his back was "acting up," in a rich Chinese robe in the rear parlor with the french windows that opened so incongruously on a bare paved yard, and the gilded brackets and the Hubert Robert views of gardens and the delicate Louis XV armchairs. Tea was served and champagne available. On days when the group was small enough, Gilbert would form his guests into a circle and hold forth entertainingly on the great and near great he had known in Paris, dazzling us with glimpses of Prosper Mérimée and Winterhalter and the Princesse Mathilde and even Victor Hugo. I wondered at times if he had not rather embroidered on some fairly casual acquaintances, but I reminded myself that he had remained abroad five years after I had returned and that few celebrities are immune to the grasp of a sufficiently determined social climber.

I certainly noted, in any case, the common denominator to his tales: they all tended to illustrate his resolution that the full glory of the Union triumph should be reflected in the Gallic capital. Gilbert would refer quite openly now to the "wretched back" that had kept him "out of uniform" and how, as a kind of compensation, he had dedicated his every waking hour, his every scrap of energy, to spreading the gospel of emancipation among the heathen of the Second Empire. Had Mérimée ventured to criticize the ruthlessness of Sherman's march to the sea? Oh, but how quickly our Gilbert had enlightened the author of *Carmen* and *Colomba* as to the necessity of cutting the wicked Confederacy in two and ending the carnage so much earlier! Had Hugo for a moment questioned the military occupation of the Southern states after their defeat? Gilbert had soon convinced him of the efficacy of reeducating these shattered political entities in the doctrines of a true democracy.

His mannerisms and affectations intensified with his growing cult. He was rapidly becoming an institution in the social life of the city. His body filled out; he was frankly now a fat man; his skin softened; his jowls drooped; his eyes glinted mischievously. His scarfs and robes became richer and more colorful. He took up needlepoint; he said it distracted him from his back pains, and soon he was never without his needles and materials, working away as he smoked and chatted right through his receptions, even on days when his back had not "spared him."

I began to feel increasing impatience at his extravagant demonstrations of patriotism, and one day, to the mild embarrassment of his circle, I took open issue with one of his statements, overheard when he had thought me occupied with one of his mother's friends in her old corner of the room, that he would have come home during the war, at least to work for the Sanitary Commission, had he not been reluctant to expose his mother to an Atlantic crossing and the danger of raiders.

"That's really not the case, you know, Gilbert," I called across the room. "You could have taken a British or French vessel and been perfectly safe. As a matter of fact, you and I even discussed it at the time."

Gilbert reddened and said nothing, but when I was leaving the little party, he asked if he could talk to me alone for a minute. I nodded, and he reached for his cane, got painfully to his feet and led me to the empty library, asking me to close the door. Then he turned to face me gravely. Neither of us sat.

"Are you satisfied now?" he demanded in a harsh, unfamiliar tone. "Have you humiliated me enough?"

"I didn't mean to humiliate you. I was simply correcting an obvious misstatement of fact."

"Do you think I haven't known what you were up to in coming to this house? Do you think I wasn't aware of what you and Mother were cackling about when you were sitting together in that conspiratorial corner of hers? You must think me very obtuse, Lyman Evans."

"We thought you were rather overdoing the Yankee Doodle business, if that's what you mean."

"You can't bear to have anyone get the least good out of the war but yourself, can you? Anyone, that is, who wasn't in actual combat?"

"I don't understand you. What good did I get out of the war?"

"Simply your whole successful career! Where would you

have been if, like so many of our class at Harvard, you'd fought through it? Dead, most likely, or maimed for life, or mentally crippled from years of horror and exhaustion. Look how many wrecks there are, even among the survivors. And look now at Lyman Evans! Widely acclaimed for his brilliant articles in the *North American Review* on the issues of British and French neutrality, heralded in the State Department as the man who foresaw the triumph of Prussia and the fall of Louis-Napoléon, an assistant secretary of state at thirty-five and our probable next ambassador to Paris! Where would he have been without that lucky war that gave him his needed start, his shining present and his even more glorious future?"

"I've never denied my debt to it, Gilbert."

"But you want it all to yourself! You can't abide the idea that a slacker, as you have always seen me, should share its wealth. You've always been afraid that someone — God perhaps — might find our cases not too dissimilar. Might even see us as two peas in a pod! That is why you kept me out of your office in Paris. You didn't think I knew that, did you? Well, a friend of Mrs. Bigelow's told my mother that it was you who induced her husband to turn me down. And when I at last decided to join the colors, it was you who dragged me to see those terrible pictures of mutilated corpses that scared me to death and made me change my mind. Oh, I was scared all right! I own up to that. But I wasn't the only one!"

"I wanted to save you. I knew you weren't cut out to be a soldier. Was that so bad?"

Gilbert passed a hand over his eyes. "Oh, get out of here. Please get out."

I of course obeyed. In the street I too wiped my brow. So *that* was what he had been thinking of me all these years! Well, I was ready to know it. And what he believed was my long-term and consistent motive in all my dealings with him may have had some truth in it. We can never know ourselves fully. It was certainly true that I had intensely disliked the possible parallelism that the world might see in our joint exemptions from battle. But I still think I did right to keep him away from Mr. Bigelow, who would have been sure to smell out his real reason for wishing to join us, and to deter him from enlisting in an army that he would have hardly graced. And I think a good deed may go some way to excuse even a bad motive.

Needless to say, after this I went no more to Gilbert's. But I heard a good deal about him from friends and cousins.

4.

His house in the years that followed was turned into a kind of war museum. Prints of battle scenes, Winslow Homer drawings of soldiers, posters of military announcements and photographs of officers took the place on the walls of the lovely eighteenth-century French brackets and the Hubert Roberts. Rogers statue groups — Eliza crossing the ice, a slave auction in Charleston, Simon Legree raising the lash to Uncle Tom, Lincoln with his son Tad on his knee — adorned the tables and corner cabinets. And Gilbert, who had scrupulously read the memoirs of every general, Northern or Southern, held forth, at times fatiguingly, on the errors and missed opportunities of this or that military engagement.

The last time that I saw him before his sudden death of a stroke in his early fifties was at a garden party in Newport, where he enjoyed the distinction of introducing Mrs. Julia Ward Howe, the venerable author of the "Battle Hymn of the Republic," who was to read her immortal stanzas to an enthusiastic crowd of gentlemen in white flannels and ladies in Irish lace.

It was indeed his apotheosis. He was wearing a round brown porkpie hat that might have graced the head of a lady as well as his own, and over his shoulders — the day being too chilly for his scarlet blazer alone — a scarf of an amplitude that made it seem more like a shawl. His voice when he rose to speak, invoking the long past misty morn when the great Julia had been inspired by a review of the Army of the Potomac, was higher and reedier than I had ever heard it; it was in truth almost a falsetto. Nor did he hesitate to wipe away a tear as he concluded his brief but impassioned tribute to the acclaimed poetess.

The loud applause that followed was as much for him as for Mrs. Howe. Newport embraced him as the hero of a greater era. Even I clapped fervently as I conceded his achievement. He had at last acquired a totally respectable immunity from any call to the field of battle. He had turned himself into a woman.